Mind Bender
(A Miranda and Parker Mystery) Book 10

Linsey Lanier

Edited by

Editing for You

Copyright © 2017 Linsey Lanier
Felicity Books
All rights reserved.

ISBN: 1-941191-44-4
ISBN-13: 978-1-941191-44-6

Copyright © 2017 Linsey Lanier

All rights reserved. Without limiting the rights under copyright reserved above, no part of this publication may be reproduced, stored in or introduced into a retrieval system, or transmitted, in any form, or by any means (electronic, mechanical, photocopying, recording, or otherwise) without the prior written permission of both the copyright owner and the above publisher of this book. This is a work of fiction. Names, characters, places, brands, media, and incidents are either the product of the author's imagination or are used fictitiously. The author acknowledges the trademarked status and trademark owners of various products referenced in this work of fiction, which have been used without permission. The publication/use of these trademarks is not authorized, associated with, or sponsored by the trademark owners.

MIND BENDER

Book #10 in the gripping mystery-thriller series from bestselling author Linsey Lanier

A shooting. A bank robbery. A car chase. A kidnapping.
And that was just Miranda Steele's morning.
After a relaxing vacation in the North Georgia Mountains with her sexy husband and boss, Miranda Steele gets mixed up in a bank robbery that leads to a desperate hunt for a missing woman. Never in her life would she have guessed it would be *that* woman, but she can't give up now. The woman's life may be in danger, as well as the trust of Miranda's new team at the Parker Investigative Agency.
On a twisted trail of violence, kidnapping, and mind control, Miranda is forced to face a frightening question: Can someone brainwash you to do something that's not in your nature? Like rob a bank and kill everyone in your way?
Miranda and Parker are about to find out.

THE MIRANDA'S RIGHTS MYSTERY SERIES

Someone Else's Daughter
Delicious Torment
Forever Mine
Fire Dancer
Thin Ice

THE MIRANDA AND PARKER MYSTERY SERIES

All Eyes on Me
Heart Wounds
Clowns and Cowboys
The Watcher
Zero Dark Chocolate
Trial by Fire
Smoke Screen
The Boy
Snakebit
Mind Bender
Roses from My Killer
The Stolen Girl
Vanishing Act
Predator
Retribution
Most Likely to Die
Sonata for a Killer
Fatal Fall
(more to come)

MAGGIE DELANEY POLICE THRILLERS

Chicago Cop
Good Cop Bad Cop

OTHER BOOKS BY LINSEY LANIER

Steal My Heart

For more information visit www.linseylanier.com

CHAPTER ONE

She was so excited, her skin tingled.

She could feel her own heartbeat as she listened to the murmur of Friday business being conducted around her.

As she waited in the roped-off line, she bounced on her toes and gazed up at the tall glass façade of the front wall and entrance to the downtown Buckhead bank. Ten minutes ago she'd marched through those doors, her first paycheck tucked in her pocketbook under her arm.

Well, it wasn't her very first paycheck.

She'd worked all kinds of jobs back in Austin. She'd waitressed in dives, cleaned houses, even tried a little panhandling. But she'd gone to school and taken acting lessons for the past eight years, and all that effort had finally paid off.

She was in a real movie being filmed in Atlanta.

She was about to deposit her first check from the production company.

Okay, she wasn't a star yet. She was only an extra, and the part was only supposed to last a few days. But the second assistant director seemed to be taking a liking to her. He'd asked her to stay on another week, and she thought he might give her a line in one of the upcoming scenes. Who knew where that could lead? She was on her way. She could feel it. The sky was the limit. Someday, she would be a star. She always knew she would be.

She couldn't stop smiling.

Bouncing on her heels with excitement, she glanced around at the other customers waiting in line and the busy bank clerks behind the counter. The place was crowded and felt close. She could smell the colognes and body washes of the customers near her. One large man in a suit grumbled impatiently. She should have expected the bank would be busy on a Friday just before noon. Everyone was here to cash their own paychecks and go out for a good time.

She wasn't in a hurry.

She was done for the day and didn't have plans for tonight. She'd be heading home after this stop. So why was she suddenly feeling so anxious? Maybe because Drew had promised he might stop by later.

She'd only known him a week, but she really liked him. She'd met him back in Austin and he'd asked her out. When she told him she was trying to get into the movies, he said he had some connections and might be able to get her something in Atlanta if she was willing to start at the bottom.

At first she'd thought it was a come on line. But there was something about Drew that made her trust him. But leave home and go all the way to Atlanta with him? It might have been risky, but she'd decided to do it. And it had worked out. Drew hadn't been lying. Here she was, cashing her first paycheck.

She felt a hand on her shoulder. As if he'd materialized from her own thoughts, Drew appeared at her side, wearing that heart-stopping smile of his.

"Hey, honeybun."

"Hey," she breathed in answer.

He was so handsome. Tall and broad-shouldered, dressed in jeans and his leather motor-cycle jacket, his thick black hair tousled as if he'd just been on a ride. His face was to-die-for. He was part Asian and his dark exotic eyes always made her knees feel like jelly.

"Cashing your check?"

"Making my first deposit."

"We need to go out and celebrate tonight. My treat."

She bounced on her toes again. Could this day get any more perfect?

Drew touched her shoulder again and she caught a whiff of that sexy aftershave he always wore.

It smelled like honeysuckle and cinnamon—and something else she couldn't quite identify.

The man behind her stepped a little too close. Feeling suddenly claustrophobic, she glanced around at the crowd. She was uncomfortable, antsy. She started to perspire. The A/C was on, but her skin felt like it was on fire. There were too many people in here.

She heard a voice calling to her.

"Ma'am?"

Looking up, she saw the clerk standing behind the counter. A fuzzy red haze surrounded her.

The clerk beckoned her forward. "Can I help you ma'am?"

Awkwardly she stepped toward the window.

"What can I do for you?"

The clerk was wearing a ridiculous smile. She reminded her of Emmy Holt, a girl in high school who'd always made fun of her.

Suddenly, she hated that clerk. Who did she think she was, anyway?

"Would you like to make a deposit?" The woman prompted.

"Deposit?" She put a hand to her forehead and tried to think.

She couldn't remember what she was here for. She opened her pocketbook and stared down at its contents. There was a check, but she didn't remember putting it there. She saw lipstick, tissues, a cell phone—and tucked neatly beside the phone was a small handgun with a pink handle.

How did *that* get in there?

"Ma'am?" The clerk said again.

The red haze grew dark. Blue and purple clouds began to form around the edges of her vision. She felt dizzy, sick.

"Ma'am? Are you all right?"

And all she wanted was to make that clerk shut up. She reached into her purse, pulled out the gun, and fired at the woman.

The clerk crumbled to the floor as a collective scream rose from the crowd of customers.

She spun around flailing the gun at the sea of terrified faces. Suddenly, she knew exactly what to do.

"All of you," she growled. "On the floor or you'll be next."

CHAPTER TWO

Miranda Steele stretched and yawned in the buttery soft leather passenger seat of Parker's midnight blue Lamborghini. That was a nice long nap. She flexed her arms and looking up, caught sight of the big green signs for Peachtree Street and GA-400 looming ahead.

Buckhead.

They were nearly home. She almost didn't want to go back.

After a nerve-racking case that had taken a toll on both of them, she and Parker had retreated to their favorite spot in the North Georgia Mountains. For a whole week she'd lazed around with him in bed in their high-end rustic cabin. They'd gorged themselves on the country fare and made love whenever the mood struck. They'd strolled over rolling mountain trails where the magnificent fall foliage boasted a heart-stopping array of gold and orange and burnt red hues. They'd waded in a babbling forest brook. She'd even fed a deer from her hand. She was starting to really love that area.

It was healing, therapeutic. But then, Parker always knew exactly what she needed.

She leaned over and took his hand. She loved him more than she thought was humanly possible. Marrying him was the smartest decision she'd ever made.

He smiled at her. "You're awake."

As if he didn't know.

He sat behind the wheel with a commanding pose, dressed in his casual look. Designer jeans and a polo shirt in a shade of blue that made his dark hair and salt-and-pepper edges look more sophisticated than the expensive suits he wore in the office. The glow in his gray eyes made her melt.

"Yeah." She let out a sigh. "Wish we could stay in that fairytale world forever."

"I would have stayed longer."

"Yeah, I know."

The plan was to stay two weeks, but Colby had called yesterday and said Mackenzie was making a speech at the PTA meeting this afternoon—on the dangers of vaping for young people, no less.

Miranda couldn't miss that.

Parker lifted his wife's hand and pressed her fingers to his lips. Out of the corner of his eye, he stole a glimpse of her and his heart went to heaven, as it had so many times since they'd met. With her wild dark hair and her flashing blue eyes, she possessed a beauty she didn't know she had. From the first he'd been drawn to her determination, her sacrifice, her boldness. He felt a oneness with her he'd never felt with another woman. But on their last case, she had done something for him that went beyond anything he imagined. He couldn't be more grateful. Or more intensely in love with her.

If only he could pay her back by soothing her anxieties about her daughter. Not so easy to accomplish. He was worried about Mackenzie, as well.

"Are you nervous for her?" Parker said causally.

Miranda eyed him, knowing he was reading her mind. "I don't know what to feel, Parker. She's done such a one-eighty."

"Most parents would consider that fortunate."

She took her hand back and let out a sigh. "I just can't help worrying. How can she go from vaping with some guy on the school grounds and getting expelled for it, to a crusade against it?"

"She's a fourteen-year-old."

"Yeah, I guess." Or it might be symptoms of a traumatic reaction to finding out her real father was a serial killer.

Parker kissed her hand. "It's prudent to assume the best until proven otherwise." He was being clairvoyant again. He knew what was troubling her.

"I know. I know."

Maybe it was force of habit. After enduring thirteen years of an agonizing search for her daughter, after seeing her shot by that bastard of an ex-husband she'd had, after learning what a psycho her real father was, a normal life seemed too good to be true.

But she'd try.

Forcing herself to think optimistically, she glanced at the dash. Just past noon. They had plenty of time to get home, unpack, maybe even get in another lovemaking session before the meeting at five.

The ringtone on Parker's phone broke into her thoughts. It was that chicken dance song she'd snuck on there a few days ago while he was in the shower.

Parker scowled. "I wish you'd stop doing that."

With a satisfied smirk, she looked at the display on the dash and saw the caller. "Holloway? What does he want?"

"I'll find out." Parker pressed the button on the screen to answer the call. "Good morning, Detective. What can I do for you?"

Holloway's light Texas accent came through the speaker. "I'm sorry to bother you, sir. I know you're on vacation. But I need the rest of the day off."

Parker's scowl deepened. "You'll have to speak to your manager about that. Fortunately, she's in the car with me now." Parker gave Miranda a nod, transferring his scowl along with the call.

She pressed her lips together in annoyance. She'd never wanted to manage a team, especially not her old work buddy, a guy who resented the arrangement as much as she did. Besides, she knew Holloway was royally po'd she hadn't taken him along on their last case.

But the job was the job. For now.

"What is it, Holloway?" She made sure to add a touch of the irritation she was feeling to her tone. She'd given the team the option of down time before she'd left with Parker for the mountains. Holloway had opted to stay in the office. Now he wanted time off?

"I need the day off, Steele," he said, sounding as grouchy as she did.

She didn't really care if he took it off, but why did she have to be the one to say yes or no? She heard traffic in the background. "Sounds like you've already taken it."

"Actually, I have."

"Why did you call in, then?"

"Following protocol."

Protocol would be calling in *before* you left. She couldn't bring herself to point that out. Instead she said, "Okay. Why do you need the day off on such short notice, Holloway?"

Did Gen have some cozy cushions ready for them to try out at her apartment? By now Miranda was pretty sure Parker knew Holloway and his daughter were dating, but surely Holloway would have enough sense not to blurt out something like that now.

"It's an emergency."

She rolled her eyes. "The toilet flood in your apartment?"

She heard an angry huff on the other end. "I got a call from my ex-wife a few minutes ago."

Ex-wife? Holloway hadn't mentioned his ex-wife in a long time. She was under the impression they weren't in contact with each other. "What did she want?"

"There's a bank robbery in progress in downtown Buckhead. She's being held hostage. She called me for help."

Miranda looked at Parker. Bank robbery? This really was serious.

"Which bank? We'll get there as fast as we can."

"I don't need your help, Steele."

"Of course, you do."

"I've had the same training you have. I'll handle it." And he hung up.

Parker's jaw was tight as he reached for the radio.

"I'll do that." Miranda pressed buttons, scanning through country music, a talk show, and static before she got what they needed.

"We interrupt this broadcast with breaking news," said a man with alarm in his voice. "A few minutes ago gunshot broke out at the South Exchange Bank in downtown Buckhead. Police are arriving at the scene now, and there seems to be a hostage situation in progress." The reporter went on to interview a bystander who didn't know much more than what he'd already stated.

Miranda was on her phone, looking up the address. "South Exchange Bank. It's close to the office. Just off Piedmont." And near Parker's penthouse, too.

"Hosea must be there already," Parker said darkly.

Parker and Lieutenant Hosea Erskine of the APD went way back.

"Probably. Let's go."

Her stomach lurching, she watched Parker cut the steering wheel and speed down the exit, heading for Piedmont Street.

CHAPTER THREE

Every nerve tight, Miranda scanned the streets as they swung through the traffic around Lenox then onto GA-141. Changing lanes several times, they zoomed through the cars and the tangle of tunnels and twisty asphalt with creatively shaped high-rises looming on every jagged corner. They passed a bistro Parker had taken her to once, a high end shopping area, rows of sweeping glass-and-steel towers housing offices, high-end hotels, and pricey restaurants.

At last, near a gourmet eatery shaped like a glass spaceship, she spotted the commotion.

A snarled mass of cars blocked a gated parking entrance. A line of police were trying to keep nosy pedestrians and TV camera crews at bay, while more cops cordoned off the sidewalk with crime scene tape. Uniforms were everywhere.

With a loud screech, Parker pulled the Lamborghini along the curb. They retrieved their weapons from the glove compartment and hopped out.

A jangle of shouts and groans from the pedestrians, the cops, and the reporters greeted her ears. The smell of charbroiled steak in her nose and the cool autumn wind whistling through her hair, Miranda raced up the walkway with Parker, pushing her way through the crowd.

Up ahead she saw a row of police cruisers parked crossway on a brick-lined sidewalk, about fifty feet away from the gleaming glass entrance of South Exchange Bank.

She recognized the man in charge, Lieutenant Hosea Erskine, who was leaning over the hood of one of the cars, commanding his people.

Off to the side a SWAT truck sat, lights flashing. Several members of the team were cautiously moving in. Dressed in army green, complete with vests, goggles, helmets, and submachine guns, they took cover behind the cylindrical concrete columns that decorated the entrance and waited for instruction.

"Easy," Erskine said through his radio. "Slow. Nice and slow. Hold your positions. Don't let the suspect see you."

Back from the team, creeping along the concrete wall of the next building, someone with a TV camera appeared.

"Get those news people out of here," Erskine barked to one of his men. "Don't they know there are lives at stake?"

Two uniforms hurried off to take care of the reporter.

"Hosea," Parker murmured as he reached the Lieutenant.

Erskine turned to glance at Parker. He looked at Miranda, his dark marble eyes boring into her the way they did during her initial encounter with him when she'd first come to Atlanta.

He gave a short nod. "Glad to see you, Parker. You, too, Ms. Steele."

That was different. But Erskine had acted differently toward her ever since the incident in Jasper County a month and a half ago. And he and Parker had a love-hate relationship that went way back. She was glad he was being sociable right now.

"Where's Chambers?" Miranda asked. She assumed the officer who was now a sergeant and tentatively an ally of hers would have been called to this scene.

"On vacation," Erskine said.

She wondered if he'd be sorry to miss all the hubbub.

"Grab a vest and join in the fun," the Lieutenant told them.

An officer handed Parker and Miranda Kevlar vests, and they pulled them on.

"What's the situation?" Parker said.

Erskine shook his head. "Don't know much. There's a shooter and a lot of hostages. A bank clerk was shot. The shooter let someone look at the clerk, and the hostage set off the alarm to call us. We don't know the clerk's status or if there was retaliation. We haven't made contact yet."

Someone had been shot? Not good. They could be bleeding to death in there.

A dispatcher squawked through the speaker in the car, reporting the position of various units.

Suddenly a shot rang out from inside the bank. It hit the glass about twenty feet up, making a huge spider web. But the glass didn't break. It was blast resistant. Still, Miranda could hear the muffled screams of the people inside. Her heart went out to them. They had to do something.

"Hold your positions," Erskine commanded. "Do not enter. I repeat. Do not enter."

He was right. If the robber saw police coming through the front door, there'd be carnage.

One of the SWAT officers scurried behind a column closer to the entrance and peered inside. "I have eyes on the shooter. Female. Blonde. Red top, jeans."

Female?

Miranda watched the beads of sweat forming on Erskine's forehead. "You have that screen ready?" he barked to an officer working with an electronic device.

"Just about, sir."

As if he needed someone to talk to, Erskine turned to Parker. "We've got executives and staff stranded on the second floor. Luckily, an IT guy is one of them. He's trying to hook up a feed to the video cameras on the bank floor."

"Good move," Parker said.

She thought so, too.

"I think we've got it, sir." The police tech held up the tablet and dark grainy shadows appeared.

Someone handed Erskine a megaphone.

He took it and spoke loudly through the mouthpiece. "This is Lieutenant Hosea Erskine of the Atlanta Police. You don't have to do this. We want to help you. What is it you want?"

There was no response. All around was silence.

"Tell me what you want. You can call my cell." Erskine gave the number.

The tech did something to the tablet and the picture cleared.

Miranda could see the woman now with her red top and jeans. She looked to be in her early thirties. Her hair was highlighted and styled in a breezy shoulder-length cut that gave her a Jennifer Aniston look.

She stood near an empty counter. At her feet sat a crowd of people—the customers who had been in the bank when she'd gone ballistic. A man with long hair in a suit. A couple clinging to each other's hands. A young woman who looked lost and afraid. A bunch more. Maybe two dozen or more. This was bad.

The woman held a small handgun out with both hands, sweeping it back and forth. She looked scared, unsure of herself. No telling what she might do.

Someone from the floor handed her a cell phone. Erskine's started to ring. He answered it.

"Hello," he said with a gentleness Miranda didn't know he possessed.

The woman's voice came through Erskine's cell speaker. "Are you a cop?" She sounded nervous. Really nervous.

"I'm a police lieutenant, yes. What is it you want?"

"I want to talk to my husband."

Husband? Was this a domestic thing?

"And who would that be?" Erskine asked.

Suddenly there were people closing in behind them.

"I told you, sir," Miranda heard someone say behind her. "I can't let you in here. You're going to have to leave."

She turned her head in time to see her lanky colleague limping up the walkway, a female police officer snatching at his arm. He'd lost his cane, but his leg still bothered him from an injury he'd gotten on a case a few weeks ago—when he'd disobeyed her orders.

Dressed in his usual monochrome look, Holloway's tan jacket and tie were blowing in the wind and his short brown hair was sticking straight up. His face was filled with alarm.

Anger bubbled up inside her. "What are you doing here, Holloway?" she hissed at him. "You know this is a touchy situation. If you set off the robber, your ex could be killed."

Too late Erskine had already turned around. His eyes were on fire, he spoke under his breath. "What the hell is going on, officer?"

"This gentleman says he's with the Parker Agency."

Holloway ignored what Miranda had told him and stepped toward Erskine. He took one look at the image on the tablet and his face went pale.

"That's my wife."

"What?" Miranda said. "I thought you said she was a hostage."

Erskine glared at Holloway.

Parker took his employee by the arm. "Explain yourself, Detective."

Holloway pointed at the tablet. "I don't know what's going on, but that's her. The one holding the gun. That's my ex-wife, Audrey."

CHAPTER FOUR

Miranda couldn't help it. She closed her eyes and shuddered with dismay.

This couldn't be happening. But it was. Holloway's ex wasn't an innocent victim in this incident. She was the bank robber. Was he behind on his alimony payments or something?

"I want to talk to my husband," the woman on the screen said again.

Holloway wedged in between Erskine and the officer next him. "Let me speak to her."

Erskine put his phone on mute. "Do you know how to handle a hostage situation?"

"I've had training."

Miranda wasn't so sure. They had done some exercises when they were IITs, but they'd never had to put them into practice.

Not like this.

Parker put a hand on Holloway's shoulder. "Do you think you can do this, Detective?"

Holloway's face went grim. "I know I can, sir. I know her."

Parker glanced her way. "Miranda?"

Miranda's gut was in a knot. Parker wanted her to make the call? She couldn't guarantee things wouldn't go badly. But that was true whether Holloway talked to his ex or not.

The things Wesson had confided to her a few weeks ago about Holloway's marriage ran through her mind. She'd cheated on him when he was in the service. She'd tried to push him around. Then she'd left him. To say the least, things hadn't ended well between them. This could get ugly.

Still, the woman was asking for him. Maybe talking to Holloway would placate her enough to take her down. What else could they do at this point?

Reluctantly, she nodded. "Just don't say anything to set her off."

"I won't."

Erskine un-muted the phone and handed it to Holloway.

Miranda watched Holloway clear his throat as he peered at the screen. "Hey, Audrey honey."

Honey, huh? The woman seemed startled at the sound of his voice.

She looked around, waving the gun at the frozen crowd on the floor. "Curt, sweetie? Is that you?"

Miranda heard Holloway take an audible breath.

"Yeah, it's me. It's good to talk to you."

"Oh, it's so good to hear your voice. It's been so long."

"It has, hasn't it?" Holloway licked his lips and looked around the square as if searching for the right words. "What have you been up to?"

That's right, Miranda thought. Open-ended questions. Just like we learned in training.

The woman grinned. "Oh, Curt. I got a job in a movie."

Holloway blinked in surprise. "Did you?"

She got a job in a movie and suddenly decided to rob a bank? That didn't make much sense.

"I did. That's why I'm here in Atlanta."

Holloway nodded and forced a smile. "That's good, honey. Great."

He was doing well. Establishing empathy, rapport.

"Do you really think so, Curt?"

He nodded his head. "Sure, sure I do, Audrey honey."

Miranda couldn't tell if Holloway was using standard hostage negotiation techniques or he really meant it.

Holloway paused, waited as long as he could before he asked the inevitable question. "What do you want, baby?"

"Want?"

"You know. What are you doing in there?" He made it sound like he was asking about the weather.

"In here?" Audrey looked around as if she didn't know where she was. Then her gaze focused on someone on the floor beside her.

She nodded. "I want you, Curt. Why did we ever break up?"

"I don't know, honey. We need to talk about it. Why don't you come out here so I can see you?"

Suddenly her face went hard and her voice shrill. "Fifty thousand dollars."

"What?"

"I want fifty thousand dollars. That's not too much to ask, is it?"

Holloway put his hand to his forehead. He was starting to sweat. He looked to Erskine for approval.

Erskine nodded.

"No, baby. It's not too much. We'll get it for you. We'll get you anything you want. But—but don't you want to come out here and see me?"

"Out there?"

"I'm right outside."

Again she seemed confused until she focused on the same person on the floor. It was as if she was getting her cues from them. "No. I'm not coming out. I want you to come in here. I want to talk to you."

"Aw, honey. It's kind of crowded in there. Don't you want to be alone?"

Suddenly Audrey's voice became a growl. "I said, get in here, dammit. You've got fifteen minutes, Curt. Or somebody else dies." She clicked off.

"Damn," Holloway grunted as he handed the phone back to Erskine.

"You did good, Holloway," Miranda told him. She meant it.

He gave her a sideways glance and shook his head. "She's going to hurt someone. I know she is."

Erskine's face went hard. "Then we have to do something. And fast."

Holloway turned to the lieutenant. "Let me do what she wants."

"What do you mean?"

"Let me go in there."

"No." Miranda grabbed Holloway's arm and pulled him away from Erskine.

Holloway broke out of her grip and glared at her. "Why not?"

She lowered her voice. "Because I'm not going to be responsible for what that crazy lady might do to you."

Holloway waved his hands in the air. "I didn't ask you to be responsible. I didn't ask you to be here at all."

Miranda rolled her eyes. She'd wanted to keep their conversation private for Holloway's sake.

Parker stepped between them, and Miranda hoped his steady demeanor would calm Holloway down. "Curt. Let's think this through. Why do you think your ex-wife is asking for you?"

"I have no idea."

"How long have you been divorced?"

"A little over three years."

"Has she contacted you before?"

Holloway's mouth twisted. "No. Not really."

"So why would she ask for you now?"

He put his hands in his pockets and shrugged. "Maybe she's thought things through and changed her mind."

Was that hope in his voice? Didn't Holloway realize he was talking to Gen's father? The woman he was dating now?

Enough analysis. "Whatever her reason, it's clear she isn't thinking rationally," Miranda said.

Holloway's eyes bore through her. "I don't care. I have to go in there."

Erskine came over to them. "I hate to break up this Parker Agency meeting, but we have someone upstairs who can access the vault for the fifty grand. We have to get the money to her in a way that makes her vulnerable. Or at least draws her away from those hostages."

"We can use the police robot," the technician suggested.

Holloway shook his head. "You can't do that. It'll spook her for sure. I'm your man."

"No, Holloway." He was driving Miranda nuts.

"I'm the one she wants to talk to. I'm the one she's asking for. I'm the only one she trusts."

Miranda looked at Parker. His face told her he was as frustrated as she was.

She folded her arms. "The only way you're going in there is if we go with you."

"No way."

"Yes, way."

Erskine caught the gist of their conversation. "No civilians are going in there. I'm sending SWAT in."

Holloway put a hand to his head. "You can't do that, Lieutenant. She doesn't like uniforms. She hated it when I was in the Marines."

"We'll have to take that chance."

"You'll set her off. She's got a real bad temper. She's already shot that teller."

Erskine's jaw went tight as he scanned the crowd of spectators and news people gathered behind the police tape. Miranda could see the images of the evening news playing through his mind. Would they be reporting a success? Or that several people had been killed today?

"All right," he said finally. "But my men will be going in with you."

CHAPTER FIVE

They got a map of the bank's interior from the IT guy upstairs. In addition to the tall glass front doors, there were two side entrances and a back exit that lead to an alley. All were equipped with security cameras.

The plan was that Holloway would enter through the entrance on the right, nearer the bank teller counter, in hopes of drawing Audrey's attention away from the hostages on the floor. The shields on the counter would give him some protection if she started shooting.

A SWAT officer would come in behind Holloway, keeping out of sight. Meanwhile, Miranda and Parker, accompanied by another SWAT officer named Jerry, would enter through the left exit and try to get the hostages out while Holloway distracted his ex-wife.

It sounded like it would work. But it was risky.

"Are you sure you want to do this?" Parker asked as they donned helmets and checked their weapons outside the entrance.

She smirked up at him. "What better end to our vacation?"

He gave her a smile that said he'd known she would say something like that.

Erskine's voice squawked through the SWAT officer's radio. "Are you in position?"

Jerry spoke into the device on his shoulder. "Affirmative, sir."

"Go ahead as planned."

They opened the door and found themselves in a bland colored passage with beige walls and beige industrial carpet. Quickly and silently they moved down the hall, weapons drawn. Following its thirty degree bends and passing fake potted plants and tall fake-oak doors that had to be storage rooms, Miranda felt as if she were in a time warp. This hall would never end.

But at last it opened onto the mother lode—the lobby where the shooter was holding her hostages.

Miranda stopped short and pressed her back against the wall. She looked across the enclosure at Parker, who had done the same. Beside him, Jerry followed suit.

She heard a cough. Weapon at her ear, she dared a peek into the lobby.

A whole crowd of people sat on a dark blue carpet scattered among golden poles of the rope dividers, encircling the woman with the gun.

Audrey. Holloway's ex-wife.

She looked so normal. Casually dressed, sneakers on her feet, a small bag draped over her shoulder. Just a normal woman come to do some banking—and to pickup fifty thousand dollars by threatening to kill everyone in the place.

A little boy's whine echoed up to the high ceiling. "Mommy, can we go home now?"

A worried-looking woman near the outskirts of the crowd took the boy into her arms. "Shh."

Audrey jumped, swung the gun in the boy's direction. "Keep that kid quiet!"

"He's hungry. If you could just let him use the restroom—"

"I said shut up!"

She looked like she was going to pull the trigger again, but she didn't.

How many shots was that? One for the bank clerk, one for the window. Miranda squinted at Audrey's weapon. Small. Looked like a 9 millimeter. If it had the typical ten rounds, that would be eight left. Enough to do some serious damage. But what if the gun had sixteen rounds?

She glanced across at Parker and saw he was making the same calculation. Way too risky to get Audrey to spend her bullets until she was out.

Where the hell was Holloway?

Finally she saw movement in the darkness beyond the counter. In the shadows of the opening that matched the one she was in near the front of the bank, she caught the gleam of Holloway's weapon. She couldn't see the SWAT officer with him. Holloway better not have ditched him.

He began to move, slowly making his way along the side of the counter.

About two feet away from the lobby proper, he stopped. She watched his face. Even at this distance, the mixture of emotion playing over it was apparent. Worry, confusion, and a little despair.

Come on, Holloway. Keep it together.

She saw his chest expand, then he called out in a friendly tone. "Hey, baby. What's going on?"

Audrey startled, spun toward the sound, waving her gun. Miranda wondered how accurate a shooter she was.

But she didn't fire. "Curt?" she answered. "Is that you?"

"Of course, it's me, baby. Didn't I say I'd come?"

"You did. Yes, you did." Audrey grinned like a teenager on her first date. Was this woman still in love with Holloway?

"And here I am."

"Come over here so I can see you."

"You come here, baby."

She took a step in that direction, then she stopped, stepped back. Miranda tried to read her face. All she saw was confusion.

Audrey shook her head. "No, you have to come here."

Holloway licked his lips and glanced toward the window where he knew more SWAT officers were waiting outside. "But it's more private over here."

"I don't care."

"Don't you want to be alone, baby? We have so much to talk about."

"Yeah, we do." Her tone turned nostalgic.

Miranda glanced over at Parker. If he was wondering how the man who was dating his daughter had gotten himself into this situation, his face didn't show it. But Parker could be cold as ice water when the situation demanded.

"Come on, Audrey. Let's get out of here and get a drink. You can tell me about your movie."

"My movie?"

She looked like she was just about to step forward again when a man on the floor touched her leg. He had long black hair and was dressed in black leather. Miranda couldn't see his face. Was that the same person she'd noticed on Erskine's screen outside?

He'd only brushed her, but the touch seemed to make Audrey turn wild.

She pointed her gun at the woman with the boy. "If you don't get out of here now, Curt, I'm going to make you sorry."

"Mommy," the boy whimpered.

The mother took her son into her arms and turned him away from the gun. She rocked him, frantically trying to keep him quiet.

Miranda watched the color drain from Holloway's face. Then he squared his shoulders. "Okay, honey. Just let me spruce up a bit. I want to look my best for my girl."

The dialog had to be making him sick, but Miranda had to hand it to him. He was a good actor.

With his weapon hidden behind him at his side, he stepped around the corner with a big grin. "Audrey, baby."

"Curt."

They stood staring at each other for a long moment. The man on the floor in the suit looked like he was thinking about going for Audrey's gun.

"They're getting your money ready for you," Holloway said.

Miranda winced. No need to bring that up.

"My money?"

"The fifty thousand dollars."

Audrey frowned as if she'd never heard of that. Slowly she shook her head. "I don't know what you're talking about."

"Never mind. Let's go get a drink. I know a place down the street that reminds me of The Roadhouse. Remember?"

She cocked her head in a dreamy look. "Where you asked me to marry you."

"Uh huh. C'mon. Let's go." He gestured toward the door.

Audrey seemed as if she was about to comply when the man in black reached up and touched her leg again. Right behind the knee. Pressure point.

"That's not what I want, Curt. I want you." She raised her arm and fired.

Just in time Holloway ducked toward the counter. The bullet whizzed past him and hit the window with a boom, making another spider web. The hostages shrieked. Several others screamed. The woman with the boy began to sob.

Audrey fired again toward Holloway, this time almost hitting him, but he managed to scrambled back around the far edge of the counter.

"Help!" someone cried. "She's going to kill us all."

Holloway raised his gun and fired back at Audrey. He missed and the bullet went into the wall ten yards behind her.

The din of screams in the room grew louder.

What the hell was Holloway doing? You can't shoot into a crowd of hostages. Before she could think what to do, Jerry stepped between her and Parker. He pointed his assault rifle at Audrey.

"Put the gun down, ma'am. We have you surrounded."

Wrong move.

Audrey spun and fired at the SWAT officer. The bullet hit his Kevlar-protected chest and he staggered a bit. Then he recovered and aimed his machine gun, about to return fire.

Before he could, Parker grabbed the gun and pointed it at the ceiling. "There are civilians in here."

Jerry glared at him. "I'm well aware of that, Mr. Parker. I'm not going to hit one."

No time to discuss the possibility. Audrey fired again. Parker and the SWAT officer ducked back around the corridor wall just in time.

Relief swelling inside her, Miranda calculated. Six rounds spent. Did she have four left? Or ten?

She squatted down, about to exit the hall and make her way around the crowd in the confusion. Suddenly the guy in black on the floor got to his feet, took Audrey's hand and pulled her toward the back.

They disappeared through a rear opening.

Realizing their captor had vacated the premises, some of the hostages began to get up and run for the doors.

Parker rushed from the corridor. "Over here," he said, guiding them out the front where the rest of the SWAT team was.

Miranda joined him.

"They're heading out the back," Jerry said into his microphone.

Erskine's voice bellowed, "They?"

"The suspect left with a man. Long black hair. Black leather jacket and jeans. About six foot, average weight."

Shots and shouting came from the hall where Audrey and the guy had disappeared. There was another SWAT officer back there.

"Unit ten, report," Erskine cried. "What's your status?"

"Unit ten. I've been hit. Suspect and a man in black are climbing into a white van."

"Tag number?"

"Blank." He went silent.

"Get an ambulance back there." Erskine sounded frantic.

Miranda helped Parker steer the rest of the crazed crowd out the door.

He gestured to Jerry. "Can you take over here?"

The SWAT officer nodded.

Parker turned to her and pointed back toward the corridor. "We can get to the car that way."

"Right." She turned back for only a second. "Holloway. With us."

For a change, Holloway didn't argue. He barreled through the crowd of escaping hostages and was behind her just as they made the first turn into the hall.

CHAPTER SIX

Outside, they scrambled across the pavement to Parker's Lamborghini as fast as humanly possible.

Miranda hopped into the passenger seat while Parker raced around to the driver's side and Holloway squeezed his lanky body into the cramped area behind the front seats. The next instant Parker pressed the button and the sports car growled to life. He leaned on the horn to blare out a warning to pedestrians, and swung into traffic just as a couple of the cops reached their squad cars behind them.

The cops sounded their sirens, but Parker had already roared around the corner onto Piedmont.

Miranda pointed up ahead. "There they are."

There was only one white van, and it had just passed a furniture store on the left, more than a hundred yards away.

"They're heading north," Holloway said as they zoomed past a tidy row of trees and hedges growing alongside the tall buildings.

Were they headed for the mall? Miranda wondered what kind of carnage they might be planning there.

"Can we catch them?" Holloway said.

She thought she heard Parker utter a low "hah" under his breath as he steered around a Honda mini-van and an Explorer. And then they hit the post-lunchtime traffic and screeched to a halt.

"Damn!" Holloway cried.

"The traffic will slow the van down, too," she told him, trying not to sound like his mother.

But as soon as the words were out of her mouth, the white van pulled out of the line of waiting cars and into the opposite lane.

"What are they doing?" Thank God there was no oncoming traffic, Miranda thought—then Parker did the same.

She held her breath as they whizzed past the string of cars lined up on the street alongside the hotels and bank buildings.

They were closing in on the van. Only a few feet away now.

At last the two cops cars came around the corner behind them, sirens screaming. Drivers started pulling over, but that only caused more confusion.

In the opposite lane Miranda saw a bus coming straight for the van. "Look out!"

The van swung back into its lane. Tires squealing, Parker swerved and just missed the bus, an Audi pulling to the curb in time to give him just enough space to avoid a collision.

Miranda caught a glimpse of the hapless bus driver shaking his fist at them. He must be wondering what the heck was going on. No time to think about that.

The van was zooming ahead of them.

Just beyond the lane it now occupied was a construction area with orange cones blocking access. That had been part of the hold up. The van ran over the cones with a slapping sound and ploughed through the workers, sending them yelling and scurrying to the sidewalk for safety.

Now she really was mad. She used to be a road worker.

Parker was mad, too. Jaw tight, he zoomed ahead and finally caught up to the van. With another surge, he hit the rear bumper.

The van swerved, then pulled ahead, screeching as it swung around the corner onto Lenox. Too fast. The van barreled up onto the sidewalk and sent pedestrians running to get out of the way. Some of them screamed for help, others stopped and started recording the action with their cell phones.

Miranda could smell burning rubber as the curving glass of the corner building whizzed by.

Still, the commotion on the sidewalk had slowed them down. The van was maybe fifty yards ahead of them now.

Miranda felt like she could bite through nails. "Don't lose him."

"I won't."

"We can't," Holloway said. "We can't let that guy drive off with Audrey."

"Who was he?" Miranda said.

"I don't know. Never seen him before. Is he heading for the mall?" Holloway echoed Miranda's earlier concern.

They were flying down a wide road past the restaurants and coffee shops and into the tree-and-brick lined area near the mall.

"He'll hit traffic here for sure."

She was glad there was a median on this road, complete with foliage growing out of it. The van wouldn't be doing any fancy wrong-way lane changing here.

But the traffic was lighter than expected. Enough for the van to push ahead, while Parker struggled to navigate around a cluster of cars that seemed determined to slow their movement. The drivers were reacting to the police sirens, which were still well behind the Lamborghini.

It was maddening. But they managed to keep the van in sight as they puttered through the vehicles.

Miranda chewed on her lip, hoping they could stop the van before it got to the mall and took more hostages. Instead it swung around the next curve and onto the ramp to the highway, with the tall buildings of the Atlanta skyline in the distance.

"He's getting onto 400," Holloway cried from the back. "How fast can this Lambo go, sir?"

"Two-twenty on a good day. But not with traffic."

"That van can't be faster," Miranda said.

Parker's grip tightened on the wheel. "It isn't. And neither is that truck."

The shadow of a huge eighteen wheeler pulled up to their left, blocking their view of the van. They didn't have much of the ramp left before they'd have to get behind it.

"Hold on," Parker said.

He pressed the accelerator, and for a moment Miranda thought she was on a ride at the carnival. The Lambo growled and whirred like a tiger as it whizzed past the truck and into the lane in front of it. The truck's horn blaring in her ears, she resisted the urge to give the driver the digital salute.

She had other things to think about. The van had just swerved into the far left lane.

Overhead Miranda heard the chopping of a helicopter and felt a wave of relief. Then she looked up. It wasn't the police. It was a news chopper.

Just what they needed. Another appearance on the evening news.

They were going downhill now, through the tunnel south of 141, the three-lane highway dark and long and curvy. Once more Parker jammed the accelerator, and in what felt like a second the Lambo was on the van's tail.

He sacrificed the sports car's finish and turned into the van, nicking its bumper. The sound of metal scraping concrete grated on Miranda's ears as the van grazed the wall for several feet. Then it sped up again, its motor grinding as if in annoyance.

They came out of the tunnel and into the light. Miranda risked a glance in the side mirror and saw the flashing cop cars emerging behind them. Wedged between a sound wall on one side and a cyclone fence on the other, she knew something had to give soon.

"Can you get behind them?" she said to Parker.

"I can." He got into the far left lane.

"A little closer?"

"Of course." He edged up a bit until they were maybe two car lengths away.

"That's good." No need to explain. Parker knew what she was doing.

She reached for the Beretta tucked in her waistband and pressed the button to open the window. The wind whooshed into the car and whipped her hair around her face. Miranda leaned out the window, spat back her hair and aimed for the right rear tire.

She fired.

Missed. The bullet hit the van's side. The vehicle swerved and screeched, then moved across all three lanes, nearly hitting another car.

Damn. "Can you get closer this time?"

Without replying, Parker zoomed forward. Now they were one car length behind.

Miranda took aim again, but before she could pull the trigger, Audrey's head popped out of the van's passenger side window. She aimed her gun at Miranda's head.

"Don't shoot her," Holloway cried.

Her colleague was delusional.

Audrey fired. Miranda ducked inside as Parker swerved the car back to the left. The bullet whizzed past and struck the hood of the cop car that had finally caught up to them.

The squad wobbled a little then recovered.

Audrey disappeared inside the van.

"She's going down," Miranda said. "The cops aren't going to go easy on her now."

"She doesn't know what she's doing. I'm going for the tires again." Holloway leaned out the window, his weapon drawn.

"Get back in here, Holloway."

Of course, he ignored her. He squeezed off a round and blew out the van's right taillight.

"Now you've made them mad." Still it was a good shot.

Parker's face suddenly went grim. "I have bad news."

"What?"

"We're low on fuel."

She glanced down at the gauge just as a warning bell on the dash dinged. They hadn't filled up after their long trip that morning.

"If we're lucky, the police will have more units gathering up ahead somewhere." Parker was trying to be optimistic.

Miranda shook her head. "Except most of them were at the bank."

"True, but there might be one or two units who could come from the south or from DeKalb. They might be putting down spike strips."

That would be a better way to blow out the van's tires.

Someone would stop the van. They had to. But just as Miranda was envisioning what she'd like to do to Holloway's ex once the van was captured, one of the rear doors flew open. Audrey appeared in its dark cavity.

Miranda's stomach dropped. "What's she doing?"

"I don't know." Holloway sounded exasperated.

Hanging onto a side strap, her highlighted hair blowing wildly, Audrey lifted something heavy from the van's floor. The door closed again as if she couldn't manage the weight. A moment later she pushed the door open again and tossed out a long chunk of metal. A contraption that folded out, accordion-like, like a row of Z's. As the metal extended, it hit the pavement with a clang, clang, clunk.

"Audrey, what are you doing?" Holloway cried from the back.

Miranda braced herself. "Speaking of spike strips—"

"Hold on, everyone." Parker tried to swerve, but there wasn't time.

The Lambo's tires hit the metal spikes and the car veered out of control. It spun in a full circle three times and crashed into the wall next to the road, jerking Miranda around like a ragdoll. The air bags went off and nearly smothered her as they hit her in the face.

Her ears began to ring. She could feel her heart pounding through her whole body. For a while she couldn't see or hear anything. Slowly the sound of police sirens filled the air. Then Parker's voice rose above the din.

"Miranda. Are you all right?"

She heard worry in his tone. She pushed away the airbag and saw his handsome concerned face. "I think so. You?"

"Yes. Holloway?"

"I'm okay, sir."

Thank God.

Shaking all over, she climbed out of the car and saw two police cars had fallen victim to the spikes as well. A third had crashed into the second one and a fourth had crashed into the third.

Miranda craned her neck and peered down the highway. The white van was a tiny speck in the distance. So much for their valiant car chase.

Feeling numb with dejection, she turned back and gazed at the gnarled, smoking metal that was once Parker's pride and joy. The sight made her feel even worse.

The Lamborghini would never be the same.

Once again she turned to gaze down the strip of highway as the white van disappeared from sight.

Anger flashed inside her. She put her hands on her hips and muttered under her breath.

"I'll get you for this, bitch."

CHAPTER SEVEN

Soon fresh patrol cars arrived on the scene.

Miranda and Holloway talked to one of Erskine's men while Parker called for a tow truck and a cab. After they gave their versions of what had happened inside the bank and on the road, and Holloway gave the officer details about his ex, Miranda strolled back to the rear of the Lamborghini where Parker stood staring at the wreckage.

She touched his arm. "Sorry about that."

"It's just a car. I'm glad you're all right." He kissed her forehead gently.

She relished the gesture, but she knew that Lambo had meant a lot to him. She decided to try to cheer him up. "Well, you were in the market for a new car, anyway. Right?"

He turned to her with a bland expression. "Was I?"

She'd thought he was going to surprise her with a new roadster to replace the shiny red Corvette ZR1 she'd traded in after she left him a month ago. Maybe she'd been wrong about that. Maybe what she'd done had stung a little too deeply.

Holloway strolled over to them, hands in his pockets. He looked like he'd lost his best friend. "Officer Stilton's going to take me back to my car."

Holloway's Mini Cooper was still at the bank.

"You should go home and get some rest." Take the day off he had asked for in the first place.

Holloway gazed at her as if she had just grown a horn out of the top of her head. "I can't go home, Steele. I have to find Audrey."

"The police will do that. There isn't much we can do now." And when they caught her, she'd be the first one to testify in court.

"Of course, there is. We're the Parker Agency. What kind of a detective are you?"

"Holloway," Parker said with the sternness of a boss. "Miranda is right."

"I'm sorry, sir. But my ex-wife is out there somewhere. That madman's got her."

"What madman?"

"That guy in black who pulled her out of the bank. Didn't you see him?"

Yeah, she'd seen him, all right. She folded her arms. "You think he's the one in control?"

"Of course, he is. Audrey wouldn't do something like that."

Holloway didn't know that. If she hooked up with a wild guy, there was no telling what his ex might do. She was his ex, after all. Maybe she'd changed. She sure seemed in control of her faculties to Miranda.

Still, maybe the situation was worth checking out. And maybe they could come up with something the police couldn't.

"Okay," she said. "Meet us back at the office in an hour and we'll brainstorm."

"Thanks, Steele."

"Still want that ride?" Officer Stilton called from his patrol car.

"I do." Holloway turned away and trotted over to the squad with a sudden spring in his step.

Parker stepped close to her and spoke in his low voice. "Are you sure you want to do this, Miranda?"

She lifted a shoulder. "If I don't, he'll go off on his own. At least we can keep him out of trouble."

"Good point."

CHAPTER EIGHT

The tow truck and the cab arrived, and Parker retrieved the two small bags they'd taken to the mountains out of the Lambo's trunk, and said goodbye to his car.

First stop was Parker's penthouse. Parker forced her to share a couple of turkey-and-Swiss sandwiches he hurriedly slapped together. They wolfed them down at the granite counter of the sleek kitchen, then headed up the spiral staircase where they showered and changed into business clothes.

They had just finished dressing when Parker took her in his arms. "Are you sure you feel up to a meeting?"

He hadn't wanted her to take on another case so soon. He'd wanted to hold onto their vacation time, let it linger a while, even after returning home. He'd wanted her to take charge of the team, but he certainly hadn't wanted to put her through a car chase that ended in a crash. He was grateful they were both alive.

He pressed her close to him. "You've had a stressful few hours. Are you sure you don't ache anywhere after the accident?" He began to run his mouth over her shoulder.

Miranda let out an involuntary gasp at the shivers he was sending through her body. Seemed like he was the one who wanted to play doctor. If she had ached, she didn't any more. Except for him.

With a laugh, she pulled out of his arms. "You're the one who had broken ribs a few months ago. How are you feeling?"

Parker's gray eyes narrowed as if to grudgingly say, touché. "But you will slow down if you notice any side effects. Won't you?"

He was truly concerned about her. He always was. But as she often told him, she was a big girl. And though she felt a little shaken after the crash, she could shake it off.

"I'm fine. C'mon. We've got to get back to the office before Holloway decides to take matters into his own hands."

He reached for his suit coat. "Nothing worse than when someone you're responsible for goes off on their own."

He meant her and her history of doing just that. Giving him a dirty look, she grabbed her cell phone and hurried out of the bedroom door.

She'd get him back for that remark later.

It was almost four when they got to the office, this time in Parker's Mazda. As soon as they made it up the back stairwell of the Imperial Building and into the hall, Parker excused himself to go check messages, forcing Miranda to face her team alone, the sneaky rascal.

Okay, she could handle this.

Squaring her shoulders, she marched back to the lab where the group always met.

The Parker Agency lab was a spacious area, with a couple of ,rows of cubes set up for the computer guys, a testing room with microscopes and special equipment for ink and tox and trace evidence analysis, and another room within, which served as the prep area for DNA testing. It was sealed and off limits to most.

That was John Fry's inner sanctum.

In front of the cubes was an open space with a long counter mounted against the opposite wall where circuit boards, flash drives and other nerdy trappings were always scattered. The Parker and Steele Consulting team had made a habit of meeting in that spot, pulling office chairs into a circle to discuss the current case.

Today was no exception.

Except it wasn't much of a team. Fry had wasted no time in taking advantage of the week off Miranda had given everyone and was somewhere bingeing on junk food and video games, no doubt. And Wesson had gone off to New York for a shopping spree.

So it was just her and Becker and Holloway.

She found Holloway sitting in a chair, his head in his hands. Her heart went out to him.

Becker sat beside him. His dark hair curling around his ears, he stared at his friend and coworker, his big brown puppy dog eyes wide with concern. He had on wrinkled jeans and a periwinkle blue T-shirt that read, "Dad Mode Loading" with a process bar under it. Miranda had to smile. Becker was married to her best friend, who was expecting her fourth child—her first with him. The poor man was beside himself with excitement.

But happiness wasn't the mood in the room now.

She eyed the missing pinky at the end of Becker's finger and thought of Paris, of the shooting at the bank this morning, of the crash she was still shaky from, of how dangerous life could be.

Becker's face was grim. "I can't believe it was her."

"Holloway fill you in?" Miranda asked as she pulled up a chair from the counter along the wall.

Becker nodded. "He told me where he was going when he left this morning. I was the one who said he should call you. I didn't know it would turn out like that." He held up a tablet he'd been balancing on his lap. "I followed it on the news, but they didn't say who was robbing the bank." Becker turned to Holloway. "Are you sure it was her?"

"Of course, I'm sure."

"Parker and I went in with him," Miranda said. "It was pretty tense."

Again Becker nodded. "And then there was a car chase through downtown Buckhead. And Mr. Parker wrecked his Lamborghini on 400. I can't believe your ex could do that."

"That bitch tossed a spike strip onto the highway. She stopped us and four cop cars."

Holloway shook his head. "It wasn't her, Steele."

Miranda gawked at him. "What do you mean it wasn't her? I watched her."

"I mean it wasn't her fault."

"She shot at you, Holloway."

Becker's eyes went round. "She shot at him?"

"In the bank." Miranda pointed a finger at Holloway. "If she had been a better shot, you might be in the hospital right now. Or worse."

Holloway looked down at his shoes. He shook his head. "You don't get it, Steele."

She drew in a breath, trying to summon some of Parker's famous patience. "What don't I get?"

"Audrey would never do something like that."

Miranda put a hand to her head feeling a migraine coming on. "But she did."

"She isn't like that."

She sure looked like the real deal to her. "What do you mean?"

Holloway got up and paced over to the door to the testing room. "When we were married, she'd go berserk every time I drove over the speed limit. She ate the same thing for breakfast every day. Wheat Chex with exactly half a cup of skim milk. She kept the checkbook, kept track of every penny. One night she stayed up until three over a five cent discrepancy."

"Okay. So she's a rule follower." Or she was. Miranda couldn't help noting the similarity to Gen.

"Right. Never in a million years would she rob a bank. It just isn't her."

"Maybe she's changed. How long since you even spoke to her?"

Holloway put his hands in his pockets and looked down at the floor. "We split up three years and a few months ago. We texted a bit for awhile. I guess it's been about four or five months since her last one."

She blinked at him. She hadn't known Holloway was keeping in touch with his ex. "So you have her number?"

"Yeah."

He reached into his pocket as the next words came out of her mouth. "Call her now."

He dialed the number and put it on speaker.

Miranda held her breath as the phone's ring echoed against the Lab's walls. After two rings a dark, booming voice came over the speaker. "Yes?"

She recognized him instantly. "Lieutenant Erskine?"

"Ms. Steele?"

"Did we call Audrey Wilson's phone?"

"You did. She left it on the floor of the bank. We were hoping she might call to try to find it. How did you get the number?"

"Detective Holloway had it. Have you made any progress in finding her yet?"

"Not as yet. Has your team?"

"Not really. We'll let you know if we do. Sorry to bother you." And she pressed the button to hang up.

Miranda fixed Holloway with her gaze. "A rule follower who leaves her phone behind? It proves she's unstable."

Shaking off her stare he paced back to his seat and sat down. "That's not the point. It was that guy."

The one in the bank sitting on the floor behind Audrey. The one who pulled her out the back.

"Yeah, okay. If she was with this guy he's probably got some influence over her."

Becker looked back and forth between them. "What kind of influence?"

Holloway made a guttural sound of disgust. "Spit it out, Steele. You mean she's in love with him."

"Something like that. Sometimes when you're in a relationship with the wrong sort, you do things you might not otherwise do. Things against your better judgment."

Like clean up the mess after he tosses the dinner you cooked all over the floor. Or go looking for ice cream in the middle of the night in a bad part of town. But that was her time with Leon. Some women just go for the wild type, and if the guy is into criminal activity, they get mixed up in it, too.

Waving his hands in the air Holloway rose again and paced back to the testing room door. "Not Audrey. I'm telling you. That guy's got her brainwashed."

Miranda folded her arms and thought about how the guy had touched the back of Audrey's knee. She'd thought he'd been touching a pressure point. But it had been Audrey who'd pulled the trigger of her handgun. Several times.

Becker was fiddling with the device on his lap. "You mean this guy?" He held up the tablet.

A news show was running on the screen, displaying a grainy photo of a guy dressed in dark clothes. His black leather jacket was flung open, his dark hair suspended in midair around an Asian looking face as he ran. His expression said desperation. He clutched Audrey's hand, but she was a blur behind him. A surveillance camera in the back must have caught them as they were leaving the bank.

A newswoman was giving details.

"Turn it up," Miranda said.

Becker tapped on the screen and the reporter's voice filled the room as a still of Audrey from the feed on the bank floor appeared.

"This is the woman suspected of the shootings that took place early this afternoon at the downtown institution. According to eye-witnesses, the woman wounded both a bank clerk and a SWAT officer in the rampage at the bank. Both victims were taken to Grady Hospital. Our sources state the SWAT officer is in stable condition. The bank clerk was shot through the shoulder and is in critical condition, but expected to live."

At least Audrey wouldn't be going down for murder. Yet.

"The two suspects sent the police on a high speed chase down 400 this afternoon, assisted by Wade Parker and Miranda Steele of the Parker Investigative Agency." The picture switched to the news chopper's aerial view of the race down the highway. The white van swerved as it changed lanes, while Parker's Lamborghini followed close behind.

Good grief.

The newswoman reappeared. "At this time the suspect is unidentified. If you have any information about her, please call the Crime Stoppers number on the screen."

Holloway waved his hands in the air. "Unidentified? I told them who she is."

"Maybe Erskine wants someone else to verify her identity before they let the public know."

"We've got to find her, Steele. If you won't help I'll do it myself."

Yeah, she'd like to help put that crazy lady behind bars. "Okay." She turned to Becker. "Can you capture that image of the guy Audrey was with?"

"Sure can."

"That's something to start with. Run it through the facial recognition program. We can do a search for recent data on Audrey, too. Find out where she's staying, where she works. Wait. Didn't she say she was in a movie?"

Holloway nodded. "Yeah. She always wanted to act or sing. I never thought she was very good at either, but it was her dream."

Miranda remembered Wesson telling her something about that. It was why Audrey left the marriage. One reason, anyway.

"Okay. Look for movie companies shooting in Atlanta now. Porn companies, too."

Holloway's eyes blazed. "Steele."

"We've got to cover all the bases." And if that guy in the black leather jacket was a porn producer, that theory would fit perfectly.

There was a knock on the door. Without waiting for a reply, Gen stepped inside the room.

She'd softened her normally rigid look and had on a diamond patterned ruby dress with a V neck and long sleeves. With her white-blond hair and her tall, slender body she almost looked like a fashion model.

But she wasn't posing today.

Her face registered cautious alarm as she glared at Holloway. "I heard you were involved in that bank robbery that's been on the news."

Miranda remembered Gen coming to her during her last case and asking her not to send Holloway into any dangerous situations. Before she could think of something to say to cover for him, the reporter on Becker's tablet interrupted.

"Correction," she said. "The suspect in today's shooting has been identified as Audrey Agnes Wilson of Austin, Texas. Her accomplice is still unidentified. Our sources tell us Ms. Wilson was divorced three years ago. Her married name was Holloway. That information may help in locating her whereabouts." She repeated the plea to call Crime Stoppers.

Oh boy.

Gen stared at Holloway with her large dark eyes. "That—that was your ex? At the bank robbery?"

Holloway had no reply.

"Is that why you ran out of here today in such a hurry?"

"She almost shot him," Becker blurted out in an attempt to help.

"Your ex almost shot you?" Gen didn't look sympathetic. She looked like she wanted to do the same.

Holloway's demeanor turned sheepish. "Gen, I can explain."

"I don't want to hear it." She turned and hurried out of the room.

"Wait a minute, Gen." Holloway ran after her.

Becker hung his head and grimaced. "Sorry about that."

"Not your fault."

Miranda glanced at the time on the tablet. It was almost four-thirty. Mackenzie's speech. She'd have to leave soon.

"I've never seen him like this, Steele," Becker said softly. "What are we going to do?"

"We'll figure something out." Though she had no idea what.

Parker appeared in the doorway, a deep scowl on his face as his gaze followed the bickering couple down the hall.

Then he summoned up a calmer expression. "We need to get going," he said to Miranda.

"Going?" Becker said.

Miranda turned to him. "Mackenzie is giving a speech tonight at the PTA meeting. About vaping."

"Oh, yeah. Joanie told me you saw her—uh—messing around with that stuff."

Miranda didn't mind Fanuzzi sharing the details of her escapade with her husband. Becker was pretty good at keeping secrets. For the most part. Besides, it wasn't a secret anymore.

She got to her feet. "She's talking about the evils of it. Who knew?"

"That's great. I mean, that she turned around so fast. Bet you're relieved."

"Yes, I am."

"We both are," Parker said taking her hand.

She didn't mind him showing a little affection in front of Becker. They were friends, after all. "Well, we've got to run. Sorry to run out on you like this, but I can't miss Mackenzie's presentation."

"No, I understand. Believe me."

"Get busy on those searches. I'll check in later."

"Sure thing. I'll keep you posted if I find anything."

"Thanks, Becker."

And feeling a little guilty for leaving Becker to deal with Holloway, Miranda headed out with Parker.

CHAPTER NINE

The halls of Old Ferncliff Academy were decorated in fall colors with streamers and orange cardboard pumpkins and red-and-yellow crepe paper leaves. Announcements were posted against green construction paper, and a poem about seasons changing pulled the motifs together.

Fall.

It would be Halloween soon. Not Miranda's favorite time of the year. If her daughter was dealing with thoughts of being the offspring of a serial killer, it certainly wouldn't be fun for her, either.

Miranda walked with Parker down the pale blue cinderblock hallway and through the double doors leading to the gymnasium. The smell of baked goods and coffee hit her as she spied a table filled with goodies where parents and high school faculty were munching and chatting with each other.

She scanned the crowd.

Men and women in fancy suits and ties, fancy suits and scarves, or upscale business casual, who'd come from the office. The soccer moms and stay-at-home dads were in designer jeans and expensive blouses and polo shirts. The elite parents of the elite students of one of Buckhead's most elite schools. And here she was, a woman with a violent past who chased down violent killers for a living.

She guessed she was elite in her own right.

She spotted Colby, Mackenzie's adopted mother, talking to a couple at the end of a row of metal chairs. As usual, the woman was dressed impeccably in tan and brown layers accented with tasteful gold jewelry. Her short dark gray hair glistened with a rich ashen hue under the gymnasium lights.

Miranda gave her a wave.

Colby excused herself and hurried over. "Oh, Miranda. Wade. I'm so happy you both could make it. I was afraid you'd be tied up with that incident at the bank today."

"Incident?" Miranda pretended she didn't know what Colby meant.

Her eyes grew large with shock. "I saw footage of that car chase on the television. You both must have been terrified. Wasn't it awful?"

"Remind me why I hate reporters?" Miranda muttered to Parker under her breath.

"It was dreadful," Parker said to Colby. "We were relieved to hear the injured parties are going to live."

Colby pressed a hand to her chest. "Yes, thank goodness. They said on the news your car was totaled."

"I'm afraid so."

"How terrible."

Parker gave her a nonchalant grin. "All in a day's work. I'm glad no one was hurt."

Miranda bounced on her heels and glanced around the room, uncomfortable being in the limelight. Even though she felt perfectly at ease with Colby, she wasn't here to relive the harrowing details of the day.

"Where's Mackenzie?" she asked.

Colby's expression changed to a demur smile. "She's backstage practicing. I'm so very proud of her. I don't know what you said to her, Miranda. But she's done a complete turnaround since last week."

Miranda hadn't said anything to cause that. The last time she'd spoken to Mackenzie at the Chatham estate, it looked like the girl had already started that so-called "turnaround" all by herself. To Miranda, her daughter's transformation seemed less than genuine. But she wasn't going to look this gift horse in the mouth. Or burst Colby's bubble. Not tonight, anyway.

So she just smiled and nodded.

At the far end of the gym opposite the bleachers stood a stage. Curtains in the school colors of red and blue hung along the back and sides. Center stage was a podium with several chairs placed symmetrically behind it. To accommodate the audience, facing the stage about fifty or so metal chairs had been arranged in rows. Several folks had already settled in. Miranda watched a slender woman in a burnt orange pantsuit trot up the stage steps to the microphone.

"If everyone could be seated," she said with a teacher's smile, "we'll get started."

Colby squeezed Miranda's hand. "I'll talk to you later."

"Sure."

Miranda watched Colby hurry off to find her husband, then took a seat in the second row. Parker slid in beside her.

The woman at the podium introduced herself as the PTA president, then introduced the board members who had taken their seats on the stage behind her. The treasurer, the secretary, the VP of programs, the historian. She read the minutes of the last meeting and took a vote to approve them.

Then the treasurer got up and read a budget report and took more votes. Then the VP took the mic and reminded the parents of upcoming school events, the football and soccer schedule, midterms, and that it wasn't too early for seniors to start studying for the SATs.

Miranda's eyelids were drooping when at last the first woman said the words she'd been waiting to hear.

"And now we have a special speaker on a very important topic for all of us. I'd like to introduce Mackenzie Chatham, who's here to talk to us about teen vaping."

As the audience applauded politely, Mackenzie stepped out from behind the curtain and made her way to the podium. Her long dark hair pulled back in a lovely chignon at the nape of her neck, she wore a fitted cranberry jacket with three-quarter sleeves and a bit of embroidery at the neckline. The matching skirt hugged her slender form, and the coordinated three-inch high heels made her look very grownup.

The sight took Miranda's breath. Was that really her daughter?

Then the girl began to speak and her disbelief grew.

"Thank you all for coming tonight," she said smiling at the crowd as if they were her best friends. "I won't be long, but I feel you need to hear the latest findings about a troubling topic. One any of you might face in the future. Or might be facing right now."

She began with a few lighthearted stories that made everyone laugh and relax. She explained what vaping was and admitted she had almost fallen victim to it. Then she began with the hard stuff. She presented statistics and evidence. She pointed out studies showing the nicotine in some vaping devices was more addictive than cocaine. That while it may help a smoker already addicted to nicotine, it could harm an adolescent's brain. The flavors, like fruit or ice cream, were attractive to younger people, she said, but might contain chemicals that could cause respiratory diseases. She rattled off a list of other health issues.

Finally with a face beaming with maturity she added, "And that's why I'm starting a new organization here at Old Ferncliff. I'm calling it Teens Against Vaping. TAV. Our purpose is to distribute pamphlets and videos warning against the dangers I've summarized tonight. We have a Facebook page, and our new website will go live tomorrow with a button for donations. I hope you'll all support us. Thank you."

As she left the stage, the whole audience stood and applauded. Miranda wanted to pinch herself. Her daughter had the poise of a politician and the persuasive skills of a lawyer. She wondered if she'd gotten that from Oliver.

Applauding along with the audience, Parker leaned over to her. "She was wonderful."

"Yeah. She was."

The assembly quieted down, and the president dismissed everyone for the evening. Miranda smiled sadly as parents and teachers crowded around Colby and Oliver Chatham to congratulate them on Mackenzie's speech. Most people didn't know Mackenzie was really Miranda's daughter. It was better that way, but it still made her feel a little empty.

"Iris wanted to speak to us. Shall we?" Parker said.

"Sure."

Iris Van Aarle was the mother of Mackenzie's best friend, Wendy. When Miranda first came to Atlanta, she had thought Wendy was her daughter, and she'd felt a special bond with the girl ever since, though it wasn't always reciprocated. Wendy was fourteen, too.

She followed Parker over to the row where the Van Aarles stood.

"Wasn't that something?" Shelby beamed as he shook hands with Parker.

Wendy's father was dressed in a dark suit that revealed his muscular golf pro physique. The pink tie probably wasn't his fashion-conscience wife's choice, though. He was wearing his dark, wavy hair shorter these days, and Miranda suspected he was coloring it.

"Yes. Very interesting," Parker said.

"Interesting? It was fantastic." Shelby slapped Parker's arm.

Maybe too fantastic. And Mackenzie was starting a new group at school? With a website? When would she have time for that?

Beside Shelby stood his wife, Iris, wearing a red power suit. Her auburn-streaked hair and makeup were flawless as usual. She was CEO of her own cosmetics company, but both parents had cut back on their careers the past year to pay more attention to their daughter.

Iris squeezed her arm. "You must be so proud of her, Miranda."

"I am. Yes." She hesitated a moment. "Iris, how are Wendy and Mackenzie getting along these days?"

"Well, Mackenzie decided not to coach her this year, but otherwise they seem the same."

Miranda nodded. Mackenzie had told her she'd stopped coaching. She'd said she'd lost interest in it, though a year ago ice skating had been her whole life.

Iris might not be the best person to ask. "Did Wendy come tonight?"

"Oh, yes. She said she wouldn't miss Mackenzie's speech for the world. She's around somewhere. Probably with Mackenzie backstage."

"We're going out to dinner with the Chathams after this," Shelby said. "Carter's Steakhouse. Why don't you join us?"

Parker turned to her. "I think that would be a good idea."

He wanted her to eat. But he knew she might like a chance to spend time with her daughter, too.

"Sure. Just let me check on Becker."

She moved to the side and pulled out her phone. No updates. She thumbed a quick message.

Any progress?

Becker responded right away. *Nada.*

She looked at the time. It was getting late.

Why don't you and Holloway go home. We'll meet back in the office tomorrow at nine.

Okay. Curt's still talking to Gen. I'll tell him.

Still? That didn't sound good. She couldn't figure out where that guy's head was.

Her phone hummed with Becker's next message. *I'll keep an eye on the searches from home.*

Thanks. Say hi to Fanuzzi.

Will do.

Miranda put her phone back in her pocket and spied Wendy across the room.

The girl wasn't backstage with Mackenzie. She stood alone near the refreshments table focused on the cell phone in her hand. While Parker chatted with the Van Aarles, Miranda slipped over to talk to her.

"Hey, kid. Long time no see, huh?"

"Guess so." Wendy didn't look up from her phone.

The girl had on a nice pair of hip-hugger jeans, fashion boots, and a drapey tan cardigan over a peach top. Her dreads were gone, and her dark hair hung rich and full in a shoulder-length tangle of waves, with just a hint of blue dye at the ends.

"Looks like we're going out for steak together. Yum, huh?"

"Whatever." She punched at her cell.

"Are you Mackenzie's social media manager?"

That got her attention. She rolled her eyes and stuffed the phone into her pocket. She glanced around the room looking bored and a little lost.

Miranda forced a cheery tone into her voice. "So how's it going?"

Her lips drew together in a smirk. "Same old, same old."

She was too young for that kind of ennui. "You don't look as excited about Mackenzie's speech as everyone else is."

She lifted a shoulder. "I've heard it before. She practiced it for me a dozen times."

At least that meant they were still friends. "I heard she's not coaching you in ice skating anymore."

"Yeah. So?"

"Have you found a new coach?" Mackenzie had said she had.

"Yeah, but she didn't work out."

Couldn't match up to Mackenzie? That was interesting. "Are you looking for another one?"

"Not yet. I don't know. I might quit, too."

"But you love it." She used to. Both girls did. Back when Mackenzie had lived for skating, Wendy had idolized her.

Miranda eyed her stylish hair and clothes. Wendy was one for hiding her feelings behind her outfits. Once she'd believed this girl was her daughter. She loved her as much as if she were. She loved both her and Mackenzie.

Wendy looked around like she was getting even more bored.

Suddenly a sickening thought struck her. If Mackenzie really did know about Tannenburg, did Wendy know, too? It was reasonable that Mackenzie would share her deepest darkest secret with her best friend. Was the knowledge of who Mackenzie's real father was destroying both of their young lives?

Guilt began to flood her, but Miranda didn't want to lose this opportunity to find out more. "Are you upset with her about that? I mean, the ice skating thing?"

Wendy pushed her dark curls over her shoulder in a gesture that reminded her of Mackenzie. "I don't know. It's just that—"

"What?"

"You know. This time of year."

This time of year.

October. It was cold in other parts of the world this time of year. Like in Lake Placid. It had been only a little over a year ago that her daughter had been attacked there by the madman Miranda had once been married to. He'd almost killed her.

Of course. That's why Mackenzie wanted to stop coaching. That was it. Why hadn't she seen it before? She was so obsessed with Tannenburg she hadn't realized what her daughter must be going through right now. What memories must be playing through her mind.

Parker stepped up to her side. "How are you tonight, young lady?" he said to Wendy.

"I'm fine, Mr. Parker," she said robotically.

"Your parents are heading for the restaurant now. The Chathams are going to find Mackenzie and meet them there."

"We're going out with the Chathams?" Wendy didn't look very happy about that. Hadn't her parents told her?

"Miranda and I are going, too. Would you like to ride with us?" Parker offered.

Wendy shook her head. "That's okay. See you there."

And she ran off to find her folks.

"This might not be as fun as I thought," Miranda murmured to Parker as they headed out the door.

CHAPTER TEN

It wasn't. But at least the dinner at the steakhouse was delicious.

The table was classy, spread with a white cloth and elegant wineglasses. The smells coming from the kitchen were mouth-watering. The menu was vast, offering short ribs and lamb, halibut and lobster, and an assortment of salads featuring everything from candied walnuts to watermelon to lemon yogurt. And even though Miranda was worried about her daughter and Wendy, she couldn't help scarfing down a tender angus filet with baby spinach and creamy potatoes on the side.

Nothing like a shootout at a bank, a race down 400 at over a hundred miles an hour, and crashing into a wall like an Indy 500 driver to work up an appetite.

Still, though the girls had been seated next to each other, she couldn't help noticing Mackenzie didn't say much to Wendy.

Instead she addressed the grownups, adding to her speech with statistics and stories that didn't really improve Wendy's mood. Mackenzie seemed totally committed to her new cause. Miranda didn't know whether that was good or bad. But it was clear Wendy didn't think much of it. Miranda caught her rolling her eyes a few times.

By the time dessert rolled around, the adults had commandeered the conversation, and the men were buzzing about investment strategies, while Iris shared her insights for the latest winter fashion accessories with Colby.

Working on her blueberry upside down cake, Miranda felt as out-of-place as Wendy.

Both girls were like daughters to her, and she didn't like it when they didn't get along. But they were teenagers. What could she expect?

She asked about school and got shrugs and pat answers. She asked what the girls wanted for their birthdays and got more shrugs.

She knew what they really wanted. Things you couldn't buy in a store or online. They wanted stability. Friendship. Family. And the truth.

Something she didn't dare give them.

It was past ten when Miranda and Parker got back to the penthouse.

As they rode up the glitzy elevator to the top floor of the thirty-five-story high-rise, Miranda's mind went back to Audrey Agnes Wilson and her accomplice. "I told Becker I'd meet him and Holloway at the office tomorrow morning to work on the ex-wife's case. If you can call it that."

"Very well. I have some paperwork I can do while you handle that."

Tomorrow was Saturday, so there wouldn't be too many people in the office. In particular, Gen wouldn't be there.

She let out a tired sigh. "Holloway's still insisting Audrey wasn't at fault."

Parker nodded. "He thinks the man with her was controlling her in some way."

"Right. He says she's a rule-follower and would never rob a bank, let alone shoot people."

Parker frowned with skepticism. "An interesting theory."

"He wants to mount an all out search to go after her."

Parker was silent.

"Do you think he's right? I mean, can someone have that much influence over another person?"

"It's possible."

"Maybe. Maybe not."

The elevator doors opened. Feeling suddenly exhausted Miranda stepped out into the hall and stopped in her tracks.

Gen stood at the door of Parker's penthouse, still in the clothes she'd worn to the office. Her white-blond hair glistened under the lights, but her dark eyes brimmed with embarrassment.

She had her cell in her hand. "I was just about to text you," she said to Parker, shifting her weight, obviously uncomfortable. "Can I talk to you, Daddy?"

Parker gave Miranda a meaningful look. She knew he could see the hurt on Gen's face.

Miranda nodded and opened the tall oak door with her keycard.

"*Nuestra casa es su casa,*" she said as she strolled past Gen and through the entrance niche with its antique vases. Though she didn't think of Parker's fancy penthouse as her house quite yet.

With a scowl Gen followed her inside while Parker locked the door behind them.

Miranda turned and gave Parker a peck on the cheek. "I'm bushed. I'm going to go upstairs and get ready for bed. I'll leave you two alone."

As Gen made her way past the blue marble column and into the airy open living room to settle in the corner of one of the ivory sofas, he pulled Miranda close and murmured in her ear. "Thank you for understanding."

"Sure." She really did. Gen had to be as confused by Holloway's actions today as she was.

She gave his hand a squeeze, crossed the glistening mahogany floor, and quietly slipped up the chrome spiral staircase.

As she started down the upstairs hall, she could hear Gen's sharp voice from down below. "I thought I could trust him, Daddy. Why is he doing this?"

Parker's reply echoed up behind her. "It's the business we're in."

"It's not just the investigative business. It's a lot more personal than that."

"That's why I suggested the dating policy."

Miranda came to a halt. Parker suggested the dating policy?

Gen had mentioned she was thinking of a dating policy a few weeks ago, when they'd had their one-and-only training session in the company gym. That was when Miranda had discovered Gen and Holloway had been dating. They hadn't been together long. Parker must have known about it from the beginning.

And he hadn't said a word to her.

Here she'd been tiptoeing around, trying to keep Gen's secret. So much for the leverage she thought she had.

Feeling a little irritated at the revelation, Miranda marched into the bedroom.

She undressed, brushed her teeth and took a quick rinse in the shower to get the restaurant smell off. She pulled on a robe and checked her phone again. Still nothing from Becker.

Curiosity gnawing at her, she tiptoed down the hall and peeked over the banister.

Gen sat in the same place next to her father on the sofa, her hands pressed against her face, tissues in her lap. The box was on the nearby coffee table.

"Oh, Daddy. Why doesn't he love me?" She threw herself against Parker's shoulder and her sobs echoed up to Miranda.

Her heart went out to her. Gen had been kidnapped not so long ago. Gen and Holloway had started dating just after the Tannenburg case. Had Gen turned to Holloway to get over her trauma? She'd been so dismissive about the ordeal whenever Miranda had tried to talk to her.

But one thing Miranda knew. You couldn't get over an experience like that by pretending it didn't happen. She'd tried that tactic too many times herself. And throwing yourself into a love affair to escape the bad feelings didn't help much, either.

There was nothing she could do for the girl. Gen wasn't in the habit of taking her advice. Parker was her best bet now. His soothing arms could do wonders.

She tiptoed back into the bedroom. She eyed the huge bed with its blue satin duvet, its pale blue tufted leather headboard, the nightstands and dresser in matching blue marble accented with chrome.

She crossed the room and peeked through the blinds on the tall window at the heart-stopping view of Atlanta at night and wondered if Holloway's ex-wife was out there somewhere.

She pulled back the silky duvet and plugged in her phone. Just as she was about to snuggle into the luxurious sheets, the phone hummed.

She picked it up. Becker. Her heart nearly stopped when she read the two texts he'd just sent.

Got something. Not good news. Found an obit in a small Texas newspaper.
Audrey Agnes Wilson died five days ago.

CHAPTER ELEVEN

"How can she be dead? I saw her with my own eyes yesterday." Waving his long arms over his head in exasperation, Holloway marched over to the testing room door.

Miranda stood at the counter in the lab and poured coffee into the biggest cup she could find. As Holloway paced back and forth, she reached for one of the bagels Becker had brought and smeared cream cheese over it.

"She can't be dead. She isn't dead." Holloway took several long pounding strides back to the corner near the cubes.

As nice as breakfast was, she wished Becker would have waited for her to get here before telling Holloway what he'd learned about Audrey last night.

"It could be a mistake," Becker suggested, his mouth full of bagel.

"What kind of paper prints a mistake like that?" Again Holloway waved his arms over his head, his suit coat flapping like wings.

Though he wore the same bland brown colors to the office every day, he was usually the neat and tidy type. Today he looked rumpled and there were dark circles under his eyes. He hadn't slept much. Gen hadn't either. It had been after three when she left the penthouse.

Miranda took a big gulp of coffee and let it burn down her throat before she turned around. "It could be someone with the same name."

Holloway glared at her like she had grown another head. "In the same town?"

Ignoring his tone, she moved to Becker's chair. "Let me see that obituary again."

Becker stuffed the last bite of bagel into his mouth, scrolled to the site, and angled his tablet so she could see it.

Miranda leaned over his shoulder.

Audrey Agnes Wilson passed away October 16 in Georgetown, Texas. Funeral services are pending.

"Georgetown? I thought she was from Austin."

"Austin's about thirty miles south of Georgetown," Holloway explained.

Miranda sipped her coffee and studied the simple statement on the screen. "Not much information. There's no picture."

Becker cocked his head. "Steele's right. It could be some other Audrey Agnes Wilson."

"In Georgetown, Texas?" Holloway said with derision. "Its population is just over sixty thousand."

Miranda thought about her last case and how one person can pass for another. But Audrey Wilson had recognized Holloway yesterday. She responded to him like they'd had a history. Maybe Audrey wanted everyone to think she was dead. Maybe she'd suddenly decided she wanted a life of crime. Put your own obituary in the paper, take up with some wild guy, and go play Bonnie and Clyde with him. But why call Holloway? Maybe she got cold feet and wanted to be rescued? Why did she shoot at him then? Was the woman that fickle? Or did that guy have something on her?

Miranda wasn't about to share those thoughts with her cohorts.

An alert buzzed on Becker's tablet. His fingers moved over the surface. "There's an update in the AJC," he said. "Police found the white van this morning west of Avondale Estates. Abandoned. No plates. No registration. VIN number scratched out."

Miranda went to the counter to set down her coffee. "Fingerprints?"

"They're processing the vehicle."

Holloway strode back to Becker and read the report. Slowly he shook his head. "They're gone. Audrey and that guy are gone. I bet they went back to Texas. We should go there and find them."

He wanted to go to Texas? "We don't know where she is, Holloway."

"The police have road blocks," Becker added.

"And a warrant for her arrest. Once she's found they'll charge her with all kinds of things. Aggravated robbery, assault with a deadly weapon, terroristic threats, fleeing a police officer while driving recklessly, and who knows how many traffic violations."

Eyes wide with exasperation, Holloway spread his hands. "All the more reason she'd flee the state."

"She's a fugitive. Especially if she left the state." Her neck muscles getting tight, Miranda pulled out a chair and sat down.

Holloway took the chair next to Becker. "I talked to Audrey's best friend last night."

"Her best friend?"

Holloway nodded. "I call every so often, just to see how Audrey's doing. I didn't tell her about the bank robbery."

Miranda stared at her co-worker. He'd been checking up on his ex? She recalled a skip tracing exercise they'd done when they were IITs. Holloway had checked on someone he thought Audrey had been dating. Sounded a lot like he still had feelings for her.

"She said Audrey spoke to her on the phone last week," Holloway continued. "She's been on the outs with her parents for years, but now she wanted to make up with them. She even made a shopping date with her mother next week. She wouldn't miss that. She never missed appointments. She must have gone back to Austin."

"You just said you saw her here yesterday."

"But she went back there," he repeated. "She had to. It's what she would do."

He was grasping at straws.

Becker held up a hand. "I just found her website. She's got a nice headshot."

Together Miranda and Holloway moved to peer over Becker's shoulder.

There she was in a low-cut robin's egg blue top before a hazy white backdrop. Dazzling white smile. The same Jennifer Aniston haircut as yesterday. Girl next door look.

Holloway pointed at the screen. "There's a PO box for an address. In Austin."

Becker frowned. "Looks like the site hasn't been updated in a while."

So she meets a guy, drives several hundred miles to Atlanta to pull off a bank robbery with him, then drives back to Texas and goes to make up with her parents? Right.

She pointed a boss finger at Holloway. "You need to go home and sleep. Take a pill if you have to."

His bloodshot eyes grew wide with irritation. "How can I sleep when Audrey's out there?"

"That would be what the pill is for."

"She needs me, Steele. She could be in trouble."

Returning to her seat, Miranda forced air into her lungs. "Okay, let's take this one step at a time. Georgetown. Is that where you're from?"

Holloway nodded as he moved back to his chair and sat down. "I grew up there. I served as a Marine recruiter in the office there. Audrey and I had an apartment in Georgetown. She was working as a waitress—that's how we met. But she wasn't happy. She wanted to act."

"So she went to Austin?"

"She was always going into town and trying out for acting jobs. They have a lot of theaters there. She'd always get rejected though, and boy, that would put her in a bad mood. When we split up, she moved to Austin."

"Do you have her current address?"

"No."

"How about where she lived right after you split up?"

He shook his head. "We weren't speaking."

"No alimony or anything?"

"It was uncontested. There was nothing like that. Neither of us had much of anything. That was when I put in my application for the Parker Agency. I waited a year and was accepted."

Just before Miranda started working here. She turned to Becker. "How are you coming on those movie production companies?"

"There are over fifty legit companies in Atlanta and a handful of 'adult' ones. I sent an email blast to all of them. I've heard back from five. No Audrey Agnes Wilson or Audrey Holloway working for them."

"We should start calling them."

Holloway scowled. "That's a waste of time."

"Why? It's the best lead we have. If she got a movie deal here, she'd be living here. The movie company would have her address."

"Audrey was always saying she got a part in the movies. She wanted it so bad, she'd lie about it. Lie to herself, really. 'If you say it, it will happen,' she'd tell me. Yesterday at the bank, I was just playing along."

Miranda tapped her fingers on the countertop. Nice time to tell her that. "I still think we should check out film companies. She might have gotten a job. Who knows?"

"We need to go to Austin."

"Not until we finish here."

He shot to his feet. "You can stay here and twiddle your thumbs if you want to. I'm going. I already booked a flight."

Rising as well, Miranda gritted her teeth. Holloway was making her temples pound. "Let me talk to Parker before you do anything. And while I do, get started on those phone calls."

CHAPTER TWELVE

Miranda took the turn down the hall and headed for Parker's corner office.

She found him on the phone. He'd been dealing with mechanics and insurance adjusters, who probably didn't like their weekend disturbed.

As she waited, she ran her hand over the glass surface of his desk, eyed the blue-and-gray satiny tones of the décor, and the view of neighboring buildings through the floor-to-ceiling windows that spanned two walls of the office. Even after all this time, Parker's office was still awe-inspiring.

And he was as well.

Even though it was Saturday, he wore a dark gray-blue suit with an expensive sheen, and a matching pinstripe tie with a similar luster. But his handsome face was lined with frustration.

He hung up looking dejected. "The vehicle is definitely totaled."

She settled into one of the guest chairs. "Won't the insurance cover it?"

"Some of it. I'll be lucky if I recoup half the cost."

That would make a down payment on a new Lambo, she thought. But that wasn't much comfort, and it wasn't what she was here to talk about.

"Holloway's in a tizzy."

Parker's brow rose. "Is he now?"

She could see he was struggling with his role as a boss and his role as a father.

"He thinks Audrey went back to Austin."

Parker scowled. "And what does he base this on?"

"He talked to Audrey's best friend last night. Audrey hasn't gotten along with her parents for a long time and now she wants to make up with them, so the friend said. She made a shopping date with her mother and Holloway thinks she's going back to Austin to keep it."

"After attempting to rob a bank?"

"That's what I said, but Holloway insists she's there. He's going to Austin himself to check it out."

Parker let out an audible breath.

She sat back in her chair. "There's something I didn't tell you about."

"Oh?"

She had wanted to check it out further before she told him. He'd had a late night with Gen, and she knew his conversation with her troubled him. "Becker found an obituary for Audrey."

He sat up. "A what?"

"Here." She took out her cell and scrolled to the link Becker had given her. She held it out to him.

He read the entry and handed the phone back to her. "Very odd. But it could be someone else with Audrey's name."

"That's what I said. Holloway didn't think so."

Parker leaned back and steepled his hands. "What is his explanation for the notice, then?"

"He didn't have one."

"He saw her here yesterday. The woman said she got a job in a movie being filmed in Atlanta."

"Holloway doesn't believe that. Says she always told lies about having a role in a movie."

Parker stared out the window a moment and Miranda could tell the same thoughts she'd had about their last case were running through his mind.

He tapped a finger against his lip. "The police have a warrant out for her. She's probably in hiding somewhere with her accomplice."

That was the logical thing to do. But that woman at the bank was anything but logical. "I don't know, Parker. What if the two of them did go back to Austin? What if they're about to go on a bank robbing spree there? You know, a la Bonnie and Clyde?"

"You think she's playing an imaginary movie role in her head?"

"I don't know. She sure seemed pretty delusional yesterday. Anyway, Holloway is set on going to Austin to try to find her. He's already bought a ticket. I'm thinking it might not be a bad idea. I don't know if we'll find her and that guy there, but we can probably find out more about her. And that obituary." Not that she wanted to go to Texas. It wasn't her favorite place. "Can we afford the trip?"

She watched the wheels in Parker's head turn as he processed the information. Slowly he nodded. "We have some funds for pro bono cases."

But that was for clients who needed it. She didn't like the idea of shelling it out for Holloway's crazy ex.

The phone rang and Parker answered it. He listened a minute, then held up a finger. "One moment, Hosea. I'll put you on speaker." He pressed a button and Miranda leaned forward.

The lieutenant's gruff voice came over the phone. "As I was saying, we just received a shot of our suspects from a surveillance camera at Hartsfield-Jackson."

The airport?

"Do you think they took a plane somewhere?" Parker said.

"We're going over the manifests to try to determine that. The film was taken at six-fifteen this morning. We're also coordinating with TSA, but we're assuming the female suspect would have used a false identity."

Or she would have been flagged. "Where do you think they went?" Miranda asked.

"Anywhere. We're focusing on international flights. However, there's a chance she might have returned to Austin to go into hiding somewhere there. Perhaps with a relative or friend."

Miranda caught Parker's look of surprise. Good reason to make up with your folks. So Erskine's hunch matched Holloway's. What do you know.

"We don't have the manpower or the jurisdiction to follow up, Parker. Can the Parker Agency do that? We have reserve funds to cover the fee."

"Of course, Hosea. We'll get a team together and get the first flight out."

"Appreciate it." He hung up.

Miranda stared at Parker as he returned her gaze for a long moment. This case was getting stranger by the minute.

At last, she got to her feet. "Guess we have the money now. So we're off to Austin."

CHAPTER THIRTEEN

They stopped at home to throw a few things into the bags they'd just unpacked yesterday. Then they hurried to the airport in the late morning rush, and met Holloway at the terminal. They caught the next flight to Austin, which happened to be the same one he'd booked.

During the flight, Holloway gave them all the details he knew about anyone and everyone who used to know Audrey.

Audrey Wilson had been the only offspring of well-to-do lawyers who were now retired and lived in Sun City, a massive age-restricted community for wealthy residents in Georgetown. Audrey's parents had tried to push her into a law career while she was growing up, but Audrey had her heart set on acting— or singing—she left home after high school and went out on her own.

She never had the nerve to go to Hollywood, but while supporting herself as a waitress, she took acting lessons at the University of Texas and got a band together. They managed to snag some local bar gigs. Meanwhile Audrey was always trying out for productions in the theaters in Austin. Holloway met her when she was working at a bar where he and his marine buddies liked to hang out. He fell for her right away, and they were married a few months later. Audrey cut back on her career plans then, but she was never happy with a stay-at-home lifestyle. Her best friend had gotten her MFA and lived in a condo in Austin. Audrey stayed with her after the breakup. That was the friend Holloway had called last night. The one who said Audrey was about to make up with her folks.

While they were married Holloway had been closer to Audrey's parents than she was. They had liked him and he still kept in touch from time to time.

Holloway gave Miranda the friend's and the parent's addresses, and she made notes on all the details he'd given her. Hard to believe Audrey had come from money. The boy had married up.

With the time change, the plane touched down at Austin-Bergstrom International Airport in the early afternoon.

At the airport car rental facility, Miranda tried to tempt Parker into getting the Camaro convertible, but he wasn't in the mood.

"I'd like to make Detective Holloway more comfortable than we did yesterday," Parker told her.

A self-conscious finger against his nose Holloway cleared his throat. "About that, sir."

"Yes, Detective?"

"I'd like to rent my own vehicle. I'll spring for it."

Parker raised a brow. "Oh?"

"I have some personal visits I'd like to make while I'm here."

"Such as?" Miranda asked.

"My folks and some friends."

She folded her arms. "Does this have to do with the investigation?"

"Maybe. Just a hunch or two I have."

Miranda glanced over at Parker. He seemed as annoyed as she felt. But Holloway's relationship with his ex-wife was personal. Maybe he wanted to check out some of their old haunts and didn't want his bosses trailing along.

Plus, she'd do better without him second-guessing her every move. "Okay," she said. "But keep us posted. Every hour."

He nodded. "Will do."

And with that he stepped up to the counter to order a car.

Taking Erskine's budget into consideration, Parker chose a Corolla.

They drove down 71 to 130 north, with nothing on either side of them but a few other cars and a flat dry expanse punctuated by telephone wires and cell towers. From time to time, she thought she caught sight of the dark bronze Jetta Holloway had rented, but he was driving pretty fast. Parker, on the other hand, kept a steady, more moderate speed. No need to rush. Especially after yesterday's ordeal.

They drove for another twenty minutes and a few small farms came into view. Then a bit more greenery appeared, along with some signs of civilization. Like fenced in subdivisions.

After another ten minutes they passed a corner gas station. Beyond it quaint old homes and churches lined the streets. Now the place was starting to look more like a suburb in Atlanta, except the roads were flat and straight.

Miranda tried to imagine Holloway growing up in one of those houses.

"In the nineteenth century, this town was known for cattle and cotton," Parker commented offhandedly as he turned this way and that down several side streets.

"There was flood damage in the nineteen-twenties, but a dam was built to the north to prevent such a catastrophe in the future. In the seventies, community leaders restored the architectural heritage of the downtown area."

He made another turn and they rolled into said downtown district. Miranda gazed at the restored Victorian shops and the impressive three-story high courthouse with porticos, terra cotta and limestone adornments, and a triple-arched entrance.

"They did a good job," she said, drinking in the view and wondering how Parker knew all that.

It was a quaint little town. Would have been a nice place for a romantic getaway—if they weren't chasing down a crazy bank robber.

Parker pulled into a diagonal parking spot, and Miranda recognized the store front before them.

"The office for The Reporter," she said.

"The first stop on your list."

A rustic bench sat before an old-fashioned paned window, and a glass wood-framed door was centered under a blue awning.

Parker nodded out the window. "Looks like we arrived just in time."

At the office door stood a fiftyish-looking man with long dark graying hair dressed in an olive tweed jacket and an old pair of jeans. He balanced a cup of coffee in one hand while he bent over the latch to unlock it.

Miranda jumped out of the car and hurried over to him. "Excuse me, sir. Are you the owner of this newspaper?"

He looked up and squinted at her through a pair of dark rimmed glasses. Then he shook his head. "I'm sorry, Miss. The reporter position was filled last week. You can come in and fill out an application, though. I'll keep it on file."

"I'm not looking for a job."

"That's what they all say. 'I'll work for free,' they say. Everyone wants to get a leg up in the news business to get on TV. Then they leave me high and dry."

"I'm a private investigator, sir. My name is Miranda Steele." She dug in her pocket for a card and handed it to him.

The man took the card and studied it with a confused expression while Parker walked up to join them.

"This is my partner, Wade Parker," Miranda told the man.

Parker extended a hand. "Good to meet you, Mr.—"

"Flint. Roy Flint."

Sneaky way to get the man's name.

Flint eyed the card again. "You're from Atlanta? Long way to come for small town newspaper story. There's nothing that important going on right now. But you're welcome to come in."

He opened the door and switched on a light as he stepped inside.

The newspaper office was a one-room mess, cluttered with desks and books, papers and computers everywhere. The walls were lined with sticky notes and notices. Miranda couldn't tell whether they were past articles or notes for new ones.

Ergonomic chairs were at each desk, but all were empty.

"The staff works a half-day on Saturdays if there's nothing big going on," Roy Flint explained as he put his coffee down on the first desk. He spread his arms out indicating the vacant chairs. "See? I told you we weren't busy. They've all gone home."

Miranda cleared her throat. "Mr. Flint—"

"Call me Roy."

"Roy. We're looking into an obituary your paper printed recently."

"Obituary? We usually get those online." His face grew solemn. "Have you lost someone?"

"You could put it that way." Miranda pulled out her phone and scrolled to the link Becker had given her. "It's this one."

Roy studied the screen a moment. "Hmm. We normally print the funeral parlor's name."

"Can you tell us who placed this announcement?"

Roy rubbed his chin. "There's probably a record of it in our database. Let me see." He sat down at his desk and turned on his computer, which looked to be an old desktop. He sat sipping his coffee while the system came to life. When it finally did, he typed in a password. "Let's see. I think it would be over here." He clicked an icon. "No, that's not right. It's here." He chuckled and clicked on another icon. "My nephew usually does the computer stuff."

Miranda gave Parker a frustrated look. His face was grim. If this visit turned out to be a dead-end, they were really wasting time.

"Oh, wait. Here it is." He pulled up the text on the screen.

Miranda peered over his shoulder. It matched the online obituary.

Audrey Agnes Wilson passed away October 16 in Georgetown, Texas. Funeral services are pending.

Flint held up a finger. "Now I remember. It was this past Monday. Linda handled the notice. She's one of our editors. She didn't know what to do because he didn't have the details."

"Who didn't have the details?"

"The man who came in. He said he was from King Funeral Home. He said the family had requested only minimal information be printed in the paper."

"Did he say why?" Parker asked.

"No. He wasn't very forthcoming with any information. I wanted to call the home and confirm what he said, but he begged me not to. He said he'd just been hired and was afraid he'd get into trouble."

"And so?"

He raised his shoulders. "I felt sorry for him, so we took his money and printed the story."

Didn't seem like good business practice. Miranda glanced at Parker. He looked like he was wondering about that, too.

Reading their faces, Flint waved a dismissive hand in the air. "Oh, I've known Vernon King for years. He sometimes sends people over for death notices. Sometimes the family wants to keep things discreet. For personal reasons. We don't pry into all that."

Miranda was busy bringing up an image on her phone. The snapshot of the guy in black behind the bank yesterday. She held it out to Roy. "Was this the person who came in on Monday?"

Roy took one look and nodded right away. "Yes. That's him. He had on that black leather jacket. I wondered whether Vernon was getting lax in his dress code."

"King Funeral Home, you said?" Miranda asked.

"That's the place. It's right on Williams."

"We'll find it."

"Thank you for your time, Mr. Flint." Parker said as they headed out again. "You've been very helpful."

"No problem. Ms. Steele?"

Miranda turned back to him. "Yes?"

"Are you sure you don't want to fill out an application? You'd make a heck of a reporter."

She had to grin at that one. "Thanks, but no thanks."

CHAPTER FOURTEEN

As they got back in the Corolla and headed for Williams, questions raced through Miranda's mind.

Did the guy in the black leather jacket work for this Vernon King? Had King sent him with the death notice for Audrey? Had the two of them planned the bank robbery in Atlanta together? Or did King get some kind of cut for planning fake funerals? Or was it a completely different scenario?

Their destination was only two miles away. She might have those answers in a few minutes.

King Funeral Home was a sprawling beige brick building set off from a road running through a quiet part of town. It hosted a large parking lot that could accommodate maybe a hundred vehicles. Currently the lot was nearly empty. Apparently no memorials—fake or real—were taking place that afternoon.

Parker found a spot near the door and they went inside.

They stepped into a large waiting area with muted wallpaper and serene landscapes on the wall. Chandeliers and elegant chairs added to the hushed atmosphere. The air was cool and scented with the smell of carnations. Soft music drifted in from somewhere.

Through an open door Miranda caught a glimpse of someone in a large room, placing flower arrangements and leaning over a coffin. Preparing someone for a viewing. Apparently they did that well before visitors arrived.

A shiver ran through her and she rubbed her arms.

"Are you all right?" Parker asked, touching her back gently.

"Yeah. I'm okay."

She'd seen plenty of dead bodies since she'd started at the Agency, but a funeral parlor had its own kind of creepiness. It reminded her of seeing her mother in her coffin when she was twenty. And of the half-brother she'd never known in Maui.

A door down the hall opened, and a man appeared. He smiled as he spotted the pair and started toward them.

"Hello," he said in a sedated voice when he'd reached Miranda's side. "I'm Vernon King, the director." He held out a hand to Miranda.

As she shook it, she looked him over.

He was dressed in a stark black suit and crisp white shirt, accented by a black western string tie with a turquoise-and-silver clasp. Thin and pale, he looked like a Texas undertaker.

"Are you here for Mr. Douglas?" King nodded toward the open door.

"Ah, no. We're here about—"

King held up a skinny hand. "We at King Funeral Home are here to help you in any way we can. First let me express my condolences."

Miranda opened her mouth, but the man continued.

"If you would step into my office, we can discuss details. I don't like to carry on such conversations out here." He gestured toward a door around the corner.

Miranda gave Parker a shrug and followed the man. Might as well go with the flow.

The director's office echoed the décor of the entrance hall. Gold embossed wallpaper, a landscape of an idyllic farm. Another of a river where a barefoot boy was fishing. Serene.

While Miranda settled into a gold upholstered chair, she noticed the air was even chillier in here.

Parker took the seat beside her while Vernon King stepped behind his desk and opened a thick book with a white satiny cover. "We have a number of plans and services we can offer. May I ask how you're related to the deceased?"

For some reason, he addressed the question to Miranda.

"I'm not related," she told him flatly.

He looked over at Parker. "Was it your relative who passed?"

Parker leaned back in his chair as if he visited a funeral parlor every day. "No, it wasn't."

King adjusted the strings on his tie. "Well then, who is the dearly departed?"

Miranda gave him a pert smile. "Apparently, no one."

"I beg your pardon?"

Time to quit playing with the guy. "Mr. King, my name is Miranda Steele and this is my partner Wade Parker. We're private investigators from Atlanta."

King sat back as if she'd slapped him. "Private investigators? Has there been a complaint of some sort? I assure you my business is completely above board. We've been here in Georgetown for three generations."

Maybe. Or maybe the funeral business wasn't as serene as it looked on the surface.

"We've just come from Roy Flint's office at The Reporter," she told him.

He nodded several times. "Yes. Roy and I have known each other for years. He usually puts our death notices in the paper."

"So we understand. This past Monday, Mr. Flint tells us a young man employed by you stopped by with a death notice. This one." Once more Miranda scrolled to the obituary on her phone.

King took the phone in his bony hand and read it aloud. *"Audrey Agnes Wilson passed away October 16 in Georgetown, Texas. Funeral services are pending."* Aghast, he stared at Miranda. "We—I don't remember placing any such notice. I usually check them over before we send them out."

Parker leaned forward, taking in every nuance of the man's expression. "Are you sure, Mr. King? Flint said the young man was a new hire."

"Flint said the man insisted the details weren't published because the family wanted to be discreet," Miranda added.

King shook his head. "We always include the details in our notices. We don't send them until the family has made all the necessary decisions. The purpose of the announcement is for friends and family to pay their respects. Who was this young man?"

"You tell us." Miranda took back her phone and scrolled to the photo of the mystery man in black. "Mr. Flint identified this man as the person who stopped by his office."

King blinked as he stared at the photo. "I've never seen this man before."

A woman in a black skirt and jacket whisked past the office door.

"Emily," King called to her.

"Yes, Vernon?"

"Have we hired this person recently?"

She stepped inside the office and took the phone from his hand. Deep furrows formed on her brow. "No. I've never seen that man before," she said, echoing King's words.

"You didn't send him over to The Reporter with a death notice on Monday?"

"This past Monday? No. I'd remember that. I'm sorry. There must be some mistake."

No mistake at all.

With a satisfied smile, Miranda got to her feet, took back her phone, and extended a hand to the startled woman, then to King. "Thank you very much for your help."

King rose, looking bewildered. "Is—is that all you needed?"

Parker's smile matched Miranda's. "It was exactly what we needed."

"I believe him, Parker," Miranda said as they climbed back into the car outside. "King never saw that guy before."

Parker's face went hard. "Which means the man in the black leather jacket acted entirely on his own."

CHAPTER FIFTEEN

Parker decided it was well past time for lunch. His second-in-command needed to be fed.

He found a Mexican spot back on Main Street, and while Miranda texted Holloway, he ordered chicken enchiladas for her and flautas for himself.

The enchiladas were topped with a flavorful authentic green sauce and Jack cheese that was heavenly. And the plate of jalapeños Parker had insisted on for her was as hot as the other place, making the dish perfect, in her opinion. Miranda alternately stuffed bites of enchilada and peppers into her mouth while she checked her phone.

When she was half done, she wiped her mouth and tossed the phone on the table with a grunt. "Holloway's not exactly trying to get into my good graces."

"He hasn't responded?" Parker picked up her phone and glanced at the text she'd sent.

"No. And he didn't check in like I told him to. I never should have let him go off on his own." She reached for a chip and chomped down on it with a crunch.

"Yes, you should. Sometimes you need to let an investigator have their head. To make their own mistakes and come to realizations on their own."

"Or not."

He was talking about her again.

"Curt may turn up something valuable."

"Maybe. But he's missing the news. The guy who dragged Audrey out of that bank yesterday was here in Georgetown on Monday."

Parker took a sip of water. "And he impersonated a funeral home employee to put a false death notice in the paper."

"Yeah, add that to the charges this guy is racking up. But why?"

"Intimidation, perhaps."

"Maybe it was all his plan. Maybe he wanted Audrey to go to Atlanta and she said no at first. So he puts the notice in the paper to show her he means business. It worked. He got her to go with him and do the dirty work at the bank."

"It's a scenario that fits."

One that made Audrey more of a victim. Miranda still wasn't sure about that. She wondered if Audrey's parents had seen the death notice. Surely they would have contacted the newspaper or the funeral home. But Flint and King didn't know anything about that.

She picked up her phone again. Still no text. C'mon Holloway.

"I noticed you speaking to Wendy last night."

Parker had a way of noticing everything. Plus, he was trying to distract her from her phone.

Miranda swallowed a pepper without even a wince. "Yeah, she's really growing up."

"Yes, she is," he said wistfully. "Did she give you any insight on Mackenzie's state of mind?"

Parker had insight into *her* mind. He knew how worried she was about her daughter.

She stabbed at her enchilada. "Sort of. I think Mackenzie might be thinking about this time of year. It was a year ago, you know."

Parker's back stiffened. "Yes. I was wondering if that might be an issue."

She didn't need to explain. He'd been there.

Parker never would forget rushing off to Lake Placid only to find his wife unconscious, shot, and nearly fatally wounded by a mad killer. Because of that madman her daughter had nearly lost the use of her limb. He'd never forget the long hours he'd spent praying for their recovery. Begging with every fiber of his being that Miranda would come back to him. It had been a horrendous experience for all of them.

His heart went out to the young girl. "You should talk to her."

Miranda stared at her plate. "About the October thing? I wouldn't know what to say."

"You of all people would know exactly what to say to her. You went through that ordeal together."

He was right. "Yeah, maybe I will."

As she used her fork to drag a bite of enchilada around in the sauce, Miranda's mind went back to Gen's visit to the penthouse last night.

Cautiously she ventured onto the topic. "What time did Gen leave last night?"

"Late. She had a lot to say."

Miranda could imagine. "So you knew."

Parker's dark brow rose. "Knew?"

"About Gen and Holloway. That they were dating." She said it as calmly as if she were asking for the time.

Parker peered at her, seeing straight through her. "Yes, I did."

Miranda reached for her water glass. "From the beginning, it sounded like."

"I thought you had gone to bed."

She put the glass back down without taking a drink. "Her voice carried upstairs." She wasn't going to let him turn this around. "And you were the one who suggested the office dating policy?"

"I simply wanted Gen to think about the ramifications of her relationship. It turned out to be too late by then."

Still, they hadn't been together long. Gen must have fallen fast. "And you didn't tell me about it?"

"I thought managing the team would be more difficult for you if you knew."

"So you thought it would be difficult? For me to manage the team?"

"Isn't that what you keep insisting?" His handsome face somber, he shook his head. "It's not what I meant."

Miranda wiped her mouth and put her napkin on the table. "I found out about Gen a couple of weeks ago. I guessed it from the way she was acting."

"I know."

Of course, he did. He knew everything. "Why didn't you say something? Oh, right. The team." Meaning Holloway.

He turned to her. "You're right, Miranda. We should have been more straightforward with each other."

That surprised her. Parker usually was defensive about his secrets. But she had kept what she knew from him, as well.

Her shoulders slumped. She hadn't wanted to fight about it. "I understand. Really. It doesn't matter now. How are you? About Holloway, I mean."

"And his reaction to his ex-wife? It certainly puts me in an awkward position."

She got that. Was Parker his boss? His potential father-in-law? Or the father of the woman Holloway was about to dump?

If Gen didn't do it first.

She pushed her plate away. "Do you think Gen is going to be okay?"

"She's an adult. She has to make her own decisions." He sounded sad for her.

"Sounds like she's going to break it off."

"She might."

Miranda reached for Parker's hand and gave it a squeeze. "She's been through a lot lately."

"She has." If Miranda had nightmares about that dank basement in Jasper County, Gen must be having them, too. "She's strong. She'll get through it."

"I hope so."

Before she could say anymore, a bell jingled and Holloway strolled through the restaurant door.

Talk about timing.

CHAPTER SIXTEEN

Miranda waved him over, and Holloway plodded across the floor looking wearier and more haggard than he had that morning.

A waitress came over and stuck a menu in his hand.

He glanced at it and handed it back. "I'm not hungry."

"You have to eat," Miranda told him under her breath. After the words were out of her mouth she realized how much she sounded like Parker.

Ignoring Parker's smile and Holloway's scowl, she ordered him a chimichanga. From their many lunches together when they were IITs, she knew what he liked.

When his plate came, she gave him the evil eye until he'd downed it all.

He finished the last bite and pushed the plate away. "There. Are you satisfied?"

"We all are," Parker said with a wry grin.

Miranda could have sworn she saw Holloway's cheeks turn pink.

"Where have you been? You didn't answer my texts."

"I couldn't." He picked up a glass of soda and drank to avoid her gaze. "I went to see Audrey's parents."

"Audrey's parents?" Miranda had them on her list of people to visit, but she'd wanted to hit the newspaper office first.

"Like I told you, they live in Sun City. We always got along well. I figured they might know something about her state of mind."

Miranda recalled Holloway telling them about the age-restricted community with its well-heeled residents on the flight. She guessed he had a point. He'd be better able to get information out of Audrey's mother and father than two strange investigators.

"Okay—and how was their state of mind?"

"I didn't mention the obituary if that's what you mean. Besides, I think they'd call me if Audrey was—if they thought something had happened to her."

"And?"

"Her mother said they hadn't spoken to Audrey in a few weeks."

What? "I thought Audrey's best friend said she was making up with her folks. What about the shopping date with her mother next week?"

Holloway raised his hands. "Her mother said they didn't have a shopping date next week."

Somebody was playing fast and loose with the truth. "Did you get the sense she was lying? Like maybe Audrey's parents are hiding her?"

He scowled and shook his head. "They didn't act like anything was wrong."

"So they hadn't seen the obituary."

"No. They seemed perfectly normal."

Guess they didn't read the local paper. Miranda revised her conclusion that Holloway was the best one to get the truth out of Audrey's mother and father. She and Parker would swing by the community later and draw their own conclusions.

"You didn't tell them about the bank robbery yesterday, did you?"

"I didn't tell them anything. We just chitchatted. Henry took me out on the golf course to show me how his swing had improved. They didn't seem as if anything was different from usual."

She tapped her fingers on the table. "Speaking of that, the owner of The Reporter ID'd the guy Audrey was with at the bank."

Holloway put down his glass. "He did?"

She nodded. "Said he came in this past Monday to put the obituary in the paper. Said he was from a local funeral home."

"Did you check that out?"

"We did. The funeral home director never heard of him."

Holloway sat back with a bewildered expression. "So it was a fake obituary. I knew she wasn't dead."

Except she and the guy she was with hadn't been seen since this morning.

Still, he seemed relieved. He studied his empty plate for a while, fiddled with his napkin, then turned to Parker. "Sir, I'm wondering if I could have a moment to speak to Steele alone."

That remark had both their brows shooting to their foreheads. This couldn't be good, she thought. Well, if Holloway wanted to have it out with her, that was fine by her.

Miranda glanced at Parker. He gave her his up-to-you look. Right. She was in charge. But he didn't seem to think it was a bad idea.

"That's fine, Detective," he said to Holloway as if he had asked him to leave the tip.

Miranda got to her feet. "We'll just be outside."

She left Parker to handle the check while she stepped out onto the sidewalk. She strolled down a few stores to an art shop.

She turned to him, about to let him have it. Then she saw his face was filled with pain.

"Audrey and I used to stroll around these sidewalks together. That was one of her favorite spots." He pointed to an antique store across the street. Then he looked up and gestured to a second-story window in a Victorian style facade harkening back to a century of Texas history. "We used to live right up there. I checked it out, thinking she might go there. But it's been rented to a college student for over a year now."

He had been doing his job. She hadn't realized how hard it was for him.

Awkwardly he put his hands in his pockets. "I don't know how to say this."

"Just spit it out." Miranda was surprised at the gentleness in her own voice.

"I don't know what to do about Gen. This situation is so awkward."

"You don't say."

"C'mon, Steele. Help me out here."

"You think I know what to do?"

"You know her father better than anyone."

Was it Gen he was worried about or his standing with Parker?

Now it was Miranda's turn to shove her hands in her pockets. She walked with him a while under the striped awnings, past the quaint storefronts.

What could she say to him? "Do you have feelings for your ex?"

"I don't know. I didn't think so. Not until yesterday, but this whole thing is so weird."

Miranda pondered Holloway's predicament. At last, she drew in a breath. "Holloway, if we find Audrey—"

"When."

"Okay, when we find her. You know she'll be going to jail. Maybe for a long time."

Even if the mystery man in black influenced her, it was Audrey who shot the bank clerk. And who shot at Holloway. And who tossed the spike strips onto the highway that totaled Parker's Lambo and several police cars.

He looked down at his feet and nodded.

"I think you should wait to figure out your feelings until this is over."

He nodded and stared down the street. "Gen keeps texting me. She wants to know where we stand."

Uh oh.

"I don't want to hurt her."

Too late for that. But Miranda wasn't going to tell him what she heard in Parker's penthouse last night. "All I can say is—" How could she put it?

"What?"

"I've learned from hard experience that honesty is the best policy, as trite as that sounds. Be honest with her. Tell her you don't know how you feel and you need time to figure things out."

He smirked out a laugh. "Do you know how she's going to take that?"

"I can imagine." This was Gen, after all. "But it's the better alternative."

"And you know that from hard experience?"

"Yep."

He was silent a long while, no doubt thinking of when Miranda walked out on Parker and quit the Agency.

At last he nodded. "Thanks, Steele."

"No problem. We're going back to Austin to talk to the best friend. Want to follow us?"

He shook his head. "She'll respond better to you and Mr. Parker. I wanted to stop by and see my old buddies at the recruiting center."

For once she didn't want to argue with him. She hadn't had this intimate of a conversation with him in a long time. "Okay. We can meet at the hotel when you finish up there."

"Sounds good."

"*Semper Fi.*"

With a half grin and a salute, he turned away and headed for his rented Jetta.

CHAPTER SEVENTEEN

They headed south back down 130 toward Austin. The drive seemed long, and the afternoon sun was getting bright and warm.

Miranda watched Parker lean forward to turn the Corolla's A/C down. He hadn't said much since she'd climbed into the car after her private little chat with Holloway, but he had to have known Holloway had talked to her about Gen. Miranda guessed Parker didn't want to know what he had said.

She didn't blame him.

Parker was right. Gen was a big girl. She'd have to figure things out on her own. And so would Holloway. But a parent couldn't help feeling the pain his or her child was experiencing. She knew that only too well right now.

After another twenty minutes, the green trees and spiky buildings making up the skyline of the "Live Music Capital of the World" came into view. It would be fun to explore this place, but that wasn't why they were here. When they got into the city, they hit traffic—a jam that almost rivaled Atlanta.

It was after four-thirty by the time they reached their next destination. Miranda hoped that meant Audrey's friend was home from work.

Kenisha Trevino's condo was an open warehouse-style loft in a historic building off Eighth Street. With Parker at her side, Miranda stepped into a classy marble entrance and took an elevator to the ninth floor. They found the number Holloway had given them at the end of the hall.

As they approached it, Miranda heard loud dramatic music coming from the place. Orchestral music.

"Beethoven's Fifth," Parker said with an inquisitive frown.

Miranda rapped on the door and waited. No answer. The music must be too loud for the person inside to hear.

She tried again, using her version of the policeman's knock.

That did it.

The music went dead, the door opened, and a tall thin woman in safety glasses, a black leotard, and a tiger-striped work apron appeared. She removed the glasses to stare at them revealing dark brown, penetrating eyes.

With her thick dark hair pulled back in a ponytail, and her perfect copper skin shimmering in the sunlight streaming in through a window behind her, she had an angelic air. A silver bead ring was threaded through one eyebrow like some sort of badge.

Artist? Miranda thought she smelled turpentine.

She gave them a friendly laugh. "Sorry about the music. I like to work to it. Are you two new to the building?" Her voice was rich and musical as well.

Miranda ignored the neighborly question. "Are you Kenisha Trevino?"

The woman blinked at her bluntness. "Why, yes. Who—are you?"

"I'm Miranda Steele and this is Wade Parker."

Her face beamed with recognition as she nodded. "You're the investigators Curt Holloway works for, right? He said you might stop by to talk about Audrey."

Had Holloway been in touch with this woman since they'd arrived? Or had he assumed they'd all be going to Austin when he talked to her last night?

From the upbeat expression on the woman's face, he hadn't told her the exact nature of their visit. Or what his ex had been up to in Atlanta.

"That's us," Miranda said.

Then she watched the woman's eyes widen as they settled on Parker's to-die-for face.

Her smile broadened as she opened the door and beckoned to them. "Come in, both of you."

Miranda stepped into an open space with sky blue walls, huge windows, a high ceiling, and clean lines. To her right sat a living room, but the light wood floors were crowded with strange-looking shiny objects.

Big ones.

In the middle of the floor sat three two-foot-tall boulders in pale blue, pink, and yellow. Each one had been glazed with a swirling pattern that gave it a marbleized effect. Around the room half a dozen multicolored jelly fish were suspended in midair, held in place by thin wire. On the far wall, a huge white canvas was covered with irregular splashes of every imaginable hue.

The place didn't want for color.

A metal table stood against another wall. On it was a vice, a cutting tool, and lots of pliers and grips of all sorts. A drop cloth had been spread over that part of the floor and on it sat a large shiny bronze-and-silver creation with huge metal prongs sticking out from its center.

Miranda felt as if she had stepped into a sci-fi movie.

"Excuse the mess," Kenisha said, dragging one of the pieces aside and picking up tools from a multicolored sofa that looked like an out-of-focus digital picture. "I'm a sculptor, as you can see. I teach at UT, but I like to do some of my own projects here. Please, sit down. Can I get you anything to drink?"

"No, thanks," Miranda said, easing herself down on the digital couch.

When she was settled, she turned to Parker. She'd let him start the questions, since the woman seemed to be caught up in his charms.

After a perceptive glance at Miranda, he took a seat beside her and addressed their hostess. "Ms. Trevino, did Curt mention the nature of our visit?"

"No, he didn't. I'm wondering about that myself. And please call me Kenisha." She settled her lithe body into a bright blue shape that served as a chair.

"Kenisha, then. We're looking into his ex-wife's background," Parker said offhandedly. "How well did you know Audrey Wilson?"

"Oh, since we were little. We grew up together, went to the same private school as kids. Our parents were friends. Our fathers served on the city council together."

Miranda still couldn't believe Holloway's ex came from such an upscale background. Apparently her best friend did, too.

"Have you always been close?" Parker asked.

"Yes, pretty much. We roomed together at the University for a while. We were both in the College of Fine Arts. She was in the Acting program and I was in Studio Art. Her parents weren't supportive of her career choice. So she had to work several jobs to pay her tuition."

She folded her hands and looked down at the floor as if the memory made her sad.

"Did she finish college?" Parker asked, though he knew the answer.

Kenisha shook her head. "No. She married Curt and dropped out after her second year. I went on to graduate and get my MFA, while Audrey traveled with her Marine husband when he was stationed overseas. And when they came back to Georgetown, we talked a lot. She and Curt were having problems in their marriage, and she needed someone to confide in. I suppose you know about that."

"Yes. Some of it." Parker sat back. Her signal to take over.

Miranda leaned forward. "What sort of things did Audrey confide, Kenisha?"

"Well, they started fighting a lot. Curt had gotten the job in the recruiting center so they could both be near their families, but Audrey was never close to hers. What she really wanted was a chance to work on her career as an actress."

"Was she successful?"

"Up to a point. She started taking classes again, but she couldn't put the time she needed to into them. She and Curt needed money, so she got a full-time waitressing job. I know she resented Curt for that. She managed to get a few small roles in the community theatre in Georgetown. Then she started trying out for bigger parts in the more prominent theaters here in Austin. Curt didn't like that. He wanted her at home in the evenings so they could spend time together."

That didn't sound so unreasonable, though she could relate to a certain extent. "Sounds like she was losing interest in the marriage."

"Not really. She just wanted Curt to understand her. She felt she had to do something drastic. She told me she was going to tell Curt she was having an affair. I tried to talk her out of that."

So Audrey was a cheater like Wesson had told her. "Why?"

"Because it wasn't true."

Miranda blinked in surprise. Had Wesson gotten that wrong? "Are you sure of that?"

"Positive. She used to stay out late with me to make him think she was with someone else. We'd rent Meg Ryan movies. You know. *You've Got Mail? Sleepless in Seattle?* Audrey loved Meg Ryan. Sometimes she'd cry through the whole movie. But she never even looked at another man. She was trying to make Curt jealous."

"And was he?"

"Not right away. She said he didn't seem to care what she did, but I didn't believe that. Anyway, I told her not to do what she'd planned. I said she should just talk to Curt. She said she'd tried, but he wasn't interested in what she had to say. When she went ahead and told him about her affair, he blew his stack. I don't blame him." She raised her palms. "They had a big fight, and then she left him. She stayed with me here for a while, then managed to get her own place. We didn't talk as often after that. She was focusing on her career. She was sort of desperate for a break."

"Was she a good actress?"

Kenisha suddenly seemed embarrassed. "I love her like a sister, and I always tried to encourage her. But to be honest, I was never convinced she had what it takes to make it in an acting career."

"What do you mean?"

"She was always so straight-laced. She was a color-within-the-lines type of person."

"A rule-follower."

She nodded. "Except when it came to her parents wanting her to go into law. I always thought she'd make a good lawyer." Kenisha grew silent, then rose. "I need a soda. Are you sure you don't want anything?"

Miranda shook her head and turned to Parker. "You?"

"No, thank you."

Miranda could see he was taking in this information and analyzing what it might mean.

After a failed acting career, was Audrey regretting her divorce from Holloway? Or did she blame him for ruining her chances and was trying to get him back? If she'd stage an affair to make him jealous, maybe she'd stage a bank robbery. But she'd shot someone. And what about that spike strip?

It had to be more than that.

After a moment Kenisha returned with a can of soda in her hand. "I can't think of anything else to tell you." She put a hand on her forehead. "Why don't you be straight up with me now. How long has Audrey been missing?"

This lady was sharp. "Why do you think she's missing?" Miranda asked, trying to sound innocent.

"I know you're top investigators in Atlanta, in the whole southeast. You wouldn't come all the way to Austin for just a background check."

Parker decided to come clean. "You're right, Kenisha. Audrey is missing. We haven't determined for how long yet. That's why we needed your help."

Evidently the news here hadn't carried the bank robbery story in Atlanta.

"When was the last time you spoke to Audrey?" Miranda asked.

"Well, I hadn't heard from her in months. Like I said, we sort of drifted apart. But then last week, she called. She was so excited about this new guy she was dating."

The guy. That's who they needed to know about.

"New guy?" Miranda asked innocently.

"Yes," she said right away. "A guy she thought might be connected—to the movie business, I mean. She thought he was the handsomest thing she had ever laid eyes on."

"How long has she been with him?"

"Not long. Less than a week, I think."

That was interesting.

Miranda scrolled to the mystery man's photo on her phone and held it out. "Is this him?"

"I don't know. I never met him. But he looks sort of like the way she described him. Tall dark, kind of a James Dean look. And he was part Asian. I remember her saying that. She thought that was sexy."

"Do you know his name?"

She thought a moment. "No, I don't think she told me his name. We only spoke once in the last week." She checked her phone. "Yes, it was last Sunday. I think she'd just met the guy."

Met him the day before he put the obituary in the paper? That didn't sound good. It sounded—planned. "One last thing. Do you have Audrey's current address?"

Kenisha seemed surprised at the question. "Yes. It's on Ben White, about six miles from here."

She gave Miranda the address, and she pecked it into her phone. "Thanks. You've been very helpful. Give us a call if you can think of anything else, especially about that guy Audrey's been dating."

Miranda rose, handed Kenisha her card, and moved to the door with Parker.

Before they reached the hall, Kenisha stopped them. "Can I ask you something, Mr. Parker?"

Parker turned back. "Of course."

She studied the card. "If you don't even know where Audrey lives, how do you know she's missing?"

Parker nodded toward Miranda. Once again it was her call. She decided to roll the dice.

She drew in a breath and let it out. "Audrey Wilson and that man in the photo were involved in a bank robbery yesterday. Two people were shot. They escaped in a van that was later found abandoned. No one knows where they are."

"Oh, my God." Kenisha put her hands to her face and sank down into her chair. She shook her head. "No. No. That can't be right."

Miranda felt bad for upsetting her. "Why not?" she asked gently.

"Because that was the other thing Audrey told me about during our call. She'd gotten a part in a production of Our Town at the Civic. Her dreams were starting to come true. She wouldn't abandon them to go to Atlanta, no matter how cute the guy was."

"Are you sure about that part?" Miranda asked, recalling Holloway said she liked to lie about getting a role in the movies.

"Yes. I'm positive. They started rehearsals last week." She shook her head again. "You must have the wrong information. It must have been someone else involved in that robbery."

"Is there a rehearsal today?"

"Yes, I think so. Yes. Audrey said they'd be rehearsing Mondays through Saturdays."

"Do you know what time?"

Kenisha looked at her watch, then looked up at Miranda. "Now."

CHAPTER EIGHTEEN

The Civic Theater was across the Colorado River, only about two miles away, but traffic was bumper-to-bumper, and it took twenty minutes to get there.

While Parker did battle with the other drivers, Miranda busied herself on her phone, looking up information on the production.

"The director's name is Thomas Zane," she told him when she found the man's website. "He's been at the Civic over a decade. Done a lot of plays. Known for his 'innovative, yet classical interpretations'."

Whatever that meant.

Parker drove about a foot, then pressed the brake. "Let's hope he has some innovative answers for us about Audrey Wilson."

She tapped her fingers on her knee as she stared out the window at the standstill traffic.

There was Audrey's apartment to see, and Miranda still wanted to pay her parents a visit, even though Holloway had been there earlier. But she had a feeling the theater director who hired Audrey might just have those answers.

And if Holloway was right about his ex returning to Austin, Audrey might be rehearsing at the theatre this minute.

If they got there in time.

At last, they reached the tall glass building with an avant-garde curving rooftop.

The parking lot wasn't crowded. Parker got a spot right away and found a way in through a back door. After that it was easy.

Signs spaced at strategic locations along a curving bead board wall pointed them to the rehearsal for Our Town—and told them it had started twenty minutes ago. It didn't take long to find the door that led to the practice area.

Parker held it open and they stepped inside.

The space was large, big enough for an audience of maybe two hundred, with ascending rows of theater seats facing a wide bare stage. The stage itself held just a few plain wooden chairs and tables. The lights were dimmed. Only the platform near the front was illuminated. A man in a T-shirt and jeans stood on the stage. Leafing through papers, he described the actions of the two other characters.

The Stage Manager, right? Miranda remembered this play.

Her high school had put it on when she was a freshman, and her mother had let her go see it with a friend. The main character died at the end, and Miranda had thought it was depressing. And she didn't get why there was so little scenery. She'd assumed they were on a tight budget.

Before the stage, a thin man with a shiny shaved head sat at a folding table with an open laptop in front of him. He had on a yellow T-shirt, sneakers, and jeans torn at the knees on purpose. A woman on the stage came down a set of stairs that led to nowhere and began to pantomime cooking breakfast.

The man at the table shot to his feet. "No, no, no," he cried, waving his hands in the air. "This is 1901. She doesn't have an electric stove. She has to put wood into it from a pile on the side."

The actress rolled her eyes at her mistake. "Sorry."

The lithe man trotted up the steps to the stage and hurried over to the woman. "Like this. See? You take the wood and put it in your arms, then you open the stove door and push them in. Got it?"

"Yes, I think so."

"Start from the top again." He trotted back down the steps to his seat.

The man playing the Stage Manager started shuffling through his papers. Before he could find his place, Miranda stepped over to the table. "Excuse me. Are you Mr. Zane?"

He jumped, then glared up at her almost baring his teeth. "Can't you see I'm working here? Who let you in?"

Miranda gestured with her thumb. "We came through the door."

"This rehearsal isn't open to the public."

"We're not the public. We're private investigators and we're looking for someone."

It wasn't until that moment that the man noticed Parker standing beside her. He eyed him up and down and tugged at the collar of his T-shirt. "Is one of my cast members in trouble?"

"She might be."

He shook his head defensively. "I'm not responsible for what they do offstage. They're all adults. Now I have to ask you to leave." He turned away.

Miranda felt a few caustic words rising on her tongue. Instead of spitting them out, she turned to Parker. She'd let him take this one.

Parker gave her an understanding nod and smiled at the director with a serene expression. "I'm Wade Parker, Mr. Zane. And this is my partner Miranda Steele. We're sorry to bother you, but we're looking for a young woman named Audrey Wilson."

The man's thin brows shot up to his nonexistent hairline. "Oh, so that's who this is about. Might have known." He turned to the stage. "Take a break everyone."

The Parker magic.

Parker waited for the cast to shuffle off behind the rear curtain. "What did you mean, you might have known?" he said innocently.

"That young woman has been trying out for productions here for years. I finally gave into her because I thought she suited my interpretation of Mrs. Gibbs." He ran a hand over his head. "She had the pantomime down pat. Understood every nuance of it. But she hasn't shown up for rehearsals for a week. I had to bring in the understudy. She just isn't getting the stage business right." He shook his head.

So Audrey was here a week ago. But she wasn't here now.

Miranda scrolled to the photo she'd been showing people all day. "Mr. Zane, was this man ever with her?"

Zane didn't take long to study the screen. "Sure was. The last night Audrey came to rehearsal. He sat right over there the whole time." He pointed to a front row seat in the corner. "I wanted him to leave, but Audrey insisted he stay. Sometimes you have to give into the prima donnas."

Miranda smiled at the remark. Prima donna. She had one of those to handle, too. "Do you have any idea why Audrey missed those rehearsals?"

"Yes. She called me the next day and said she had gone to Atlanta with the guy in the front row. She said he had gotten her a job in a movie being filmed there."

Miranda blinked at Parker. Audrey had been telling the truth about being in the movies? Or was the guy in black lying to her to get her to go with him? Taking advantage of where she was most vulnerable? Miranda was starting to feel more defensive of Audrey.

"Did she mention which movie?" Parker asked.

"Or which production company?" Miranda added.

"No, she didn't give me any details."

"How about a name?" Miranda said.

"A name?"

"The name of the guy she was with."

"She didn't introduce him to me. He stayed in that chair the whole time, like he didn't want to talk to anyone." Zane put a hand on his head. "Wait. She said his name once or twice. It started with a D. Drew. Yes, that was it. Drew."

Drew. A shiver went down Miranda's spine. Drew had been one of Tannenburg's aliases. "First or last name?"

"First, I think. Yes, first. She said she was staying in Atlanta with Drew, but she'd be back when the shooting was done."

Oh, she'd done some shooting, all right. "Did she come back here? Has she contacted you?"

"No. Yes. I mean, she called me this morning, but she hasn't come back to Austin. She told me her role was extended, and she'd be staying in Atlanta another week. She begged me to keep the part of Mrs. Gibbs open for her."

"What time did she call?" Miranda said.

"It was around nine."

But Audrey and the guy named Drew had been spotted at the airport at six-fifteen. Was Audrey lying about staying in Atlanta? Was that guy forcing her to lie? If she and the mystery man hadn't gone to Austin, they could be in Cancun or Venezuela. Or on Mars.

"Do you happen to have the number she called from?" Parker asked. He was having the same thoughts she was.

"Yes." Zane reached into his pocket for his phone. "It's right here."

Miranda watched Parker's face and knew he was memorizing the number.

Parker handed the phone back to the man, then gave him his business card. "If she calls again, would you be so kind as to let us know?"

"Sure. Of course." The director's face suddenly showed some concern for his former actress. "Is Audrey in trouble?"

She might be in a whole lot of trouble if the guy in black was what she thought he was. Suddenly Miranda wanted to protect the woman's career hopes. Not that Audrey Wilson would be coming back here to play the role of Mrs. Gibbs. When she was caught, she'd be going to jail.

"We're not sure yet," she told the man and extended her hand. "Thank you for your time, Mr. Zane. You've been very helpful."

As they turned and made their way past the seats, she heard the director getting back to work.

"C'mon, people. This play is about connections. About life and death. About cherishing every moment. Let's try to get that across."

Cherishing every moment. How many moments were left for Audrey Wilson?

CHAPTER NINETEEN

Miranda climbed into the Corolla and watched Parker deftly punch keys on his phone. She knew what he was doing. Keying the number Audrey had used to call Zane into his tracker app.

He pressed the final key and waited for a connection.

Miranda thought of calling the number Holloway had for Audrey yesterday and getting Erskine. "She must have gotten another phone," she said.

"Probably a prepaid." Parker's voice was dark.

"Will that work with the app?"

"Possibly."

While the circles spun on Parker's phone, she sat back and laid her head against the headrest.

Was Audrey Wilson a victim in all this? Hard to believe the woman who'd fired several shots at South Exchange Bank yesterday, and who'd tossed spike strips onto the highway that destroyed several cop cars and Parker's Lamborghini was passive. Was she doing it for attention?

Do something outlandish, go to jail, write a book about it, become famous. Was that her scheme? But she'd just landed the role in Our Town, something she'd been striving for for years. Maybe she didn't like the part. Maybe she wanted to play the young girl instead. Maybe the mystery man had convinced her he knew a shortcut to fame and fortune.

Too many unanswered questions. Her head was starting to ache with them when Parker's phone beeped.

She sat up. "What is it?"

His face was hard as granite as he handed the phone to her. "Her cell is turned off, but this is where she placed the call to Zane this morning."

She stared at the map on the screen. Her heart started to pound with anger. "She's in Atlanta."

"On the east side."

She studied the orange dot on the map indicating the location. "That's only about six or so miles from Avondale Estates, right?"

Parker nodded. "Where the white van was abandoned yesterday."

Miranda pressed a palm to her temple. "What were they doing at the airport? Trying to throw us off the scent?"

"Making us believe they went back to Austin."

And just like a hound on the scent of a rabbit, off she went. She felt like a dupe. "We've got to get back to Atlanta."

Parker started the car. "As soon as possible."

"I'll get hold of Holloway and tell him to meet us at the airport."

She called him. Luckily he was in his rented Jetta on 130, almost back to the city. As he told her he'd stay on the highway and meet them at the terminal in thirty minutes, Miranda could hear the anxiety in his voice.

She hung up and stared out the window as Parker whipped around a Sysco truck, changed lanes and made the turn onto Riverside.

"At least we saved Erskine the cost of a hotel."

CHAPTER TWENTY

Just before boarding the flight back to Atlanta, Parker called Erskine and filled him in on what they'd learned. The lieutenant said he'd round up another SWAT team and check out the location where Audrey had made the call to Zane that morning.

Miranda wished they could take a supersonic jet to get there in time to go with them.

Instead, they landed at Hartsfield International a little after eight-thirty in the evening. The sun had gone down hours ago and dropped the temperature low enough for a blast of cold moist air to hit Miranda in the face as she hurried across the parking lot with Parker on one side and Holloway on the other.

It had rained, making the roads sloppy.

Holloway had taken MARTA to the airport from his apartment, so Miranda told him to get in the backseat with his duffle bag.

Her heart in her mouth, she listened to the whooshing of tires and watched the Mazda's headlights veer in and out of the traffic as Parker raced over the shimmering wet pavement on I-85. He turned onto I-20, and after another ten minutes they reached Memorial. They zipped past a Family Dollar, a package shop, and then Parker turned left into a huge parking lot.

He came to a halt in the middle of it.

Miranda looked up at a large rusted out metal framework where store signs had once been displayed. Under the buzzing lampposts, she could make out a strip of a dozen shops along the edge of the property lined up in a row set back from the road.

Every store was dark.

The parking lot could hold maybe a hundred and fifty vehicles, but the only ones here now were cop cars.

"It's abandoned," she whispered, dismay tightening her throat.

"So it seems."

Holloway leaned in from the backseat. "Are you sure this is the right place?"

Parker scrolled to the map his tracker app had produced and handed the phone to Holloway.

He stared at it a long time.

Miranda craned her neck to study it as well. "It's pointing to this side of the street."

Holloway handed the phone back. "Maybe they pulled in here when Audrey made the call. It was hours ago."

He might be right. Why would they stop for long and risk being seen? Or tracked like this? They were on the run. On the other hand, one of those vacant stores would be a good place to hide.

Holloway gazed across the street at the residential homes. "Maybe she's in one of those houses."

Parker rolled over to where a cluster of uniforms stood and stopped the car. Spotting Erskine, Miranda got out and trotted over to him, rubbing her arms against the chilly air.

Erskine nodded solemnly when he saw them approach. "Ms. Steele, Parker, Detective Holloway."

"Good evening, Hosea," Parker said.

Holloway broke in. "What have you got so far, Lieutenant? Have you found her?"

Erskine studied the detective a moment, taking in his distraught and disheveled condition. Then he turned to Parker. "My men and I arrived here about thirty minutes after your call. We got a key from the owner and have been checking all the stores. No trace of anyone."

Miranda's heart sank down to a pothole in the pavement.

Holloway waved a long arm toward the road. "What about the surrounding area, Lieutenant? There are plenty of houses along these streets."

Erskine nodded. "I have a team canvassing the area house-to-house."

Parker turned to her. "Miranda?"

Her call. Pursing her lips, she squinted at what she could see of the surroundings under the streetlights. Rows of small clapboard and brick houses spaced unevenly within fairly well-kept lawns. A church down on the corner. A red-brick two-story apartment down the other way. Two police officers were heading up the steps of one house, another cop and his partner moving toward the church.

No sense questioning all the residents along with the police.

"Let's go through some of these shops again. Maybe the officers missed something. No offense," she said to Erskine.

"My people are thorough, but you're welcome to look."

They got flashlights and hardhats and booties from one of the uniforms and started at the far end.

The place was a mess. Must have been vacant several years, and the tenants didn't bother to clean up when they left.

In the dim light Miranda picked her way around piles of broken sheetrock, rotting beams, and stray pipes. Everything was covered in cobwebs and at least an inch of dust. The cool damp air had a moldy smell that reminded her of that house in Jasper County.

Didn't need to dwell on that now. Stubbornly she pushed the thought away and focused as they moved to the next unit. They went through the compartments one by one.

A space that had been one of the smaller stores now featured peeling wallpaper, rusted window panes, and a ratty reception area. In a back room, they found a desk somebody had left behind with broken drawers yawning open. Might have been a dental office long ago.

They moved in and out of the doors, finding remnants of a jewelry store, a hair salon, a dry cleaner, but no signs of recent life.

At the end of the row of shops stood the last unit. The biggest by far, it must have been the anchor store of the shopping center.

Their footsteps echoed as they slowly inched through the large space. The high ceiling was supported by concrete beams that had once been used to divide the store into sections. Watch out for booby traps, Miranda thought as she dodged broken floor tiles and another pile of wood and sheetrock scraps.

Covered with dust, a sagging mattress lay on a broken frame as if too tired to care. It hadn't been slept in lately. At its foot was a turned-over nightstand with a fallen bookshelf resting on it. About ten feet away stood a couch that would send up a cloud of dust if you dared to sit on it.

Furniture store.

There were a lot more couches and mattresses strewn along the far walls. Good place to sleep if you're on the run. But there was no vehicle in the lot. Might have parked somewhere nearby and walked. Maybe in the back? On the other hand if someone had been here, there would be some sign of life. Footprints. An empty glass or bottle. A fast food bag. Something.

But as Miranda made her way toward the back of the store, she saw nothing like that. No one had been here in a very long time.

She was about to turn back when she spotted a set of overhead doors that must have been used for a loading dock. A few feet away was a regular door she supposed led to the rear area of the mall.

She turned the knob. Locked.

She took the key Erskine had given her out of her pocket, opened the door, and stepped out into the night air. It had gotten even chillier while they'd been searching through the stores.

To her left a small concrete ramp with an iron rail descended from the loading doors to a stretch of pavement wide enough for one truck. Beyond the asphalt stood a cyclone fence. A slope of grassy weeds led to the highway on the other side. Mounted wall lamps with rusted metal grids illuminated the grungy brick wall that was the back of the building. It was scrawled with the obligatory graffiti.

Making her way along the wall, Miranda ran her flashlight over the pavement. No car or truck or van here now.

A trash bag floated past her feet and into a dirty puddle. A deserted shopping cart was jammed cockeyed against the bricks. Scattered beer cans and broken bottles pointed the way to a rusty green dumpster like a reveler's breadcrumbs.

Suddenly a chill went through her. It wasn't from wind.

Something odd lay on the ground a few feet away. Carefully she inched toward the far corner of the dumpster. She stopped as she came to it, staring down, unable to believe her own eyes.

She crouched to get a better look. Her stomach started to churn. Her eyes hadn't been lying to her.

It was a toe. A severed big toe.

Dried blood had coagulated along the nail, and the skin where it had been removed was jagged and bloody. It wasn't a clean cut. Looked like it had been hacked off with something not quite sharp enough for the job.

Her temples pounded with heat, then cold. She shivered with a surge of nausea rather than a chill. Her mind reeled, whirling back to Paris. She'd never forget the sight of Becker's fingertip in that pastry box. Never forget what he'd gone through. What they'd all gone through.

But it was no good reliving the past now.

Did this toe mean Audrey was alive? And if not, where was the rest of the body?

As she was eyeing the dumpster and wondering whether she'd have to climb down into it, she heard the door creak behind her.

She turned and saw Parker frowning at her in the dim light.

"Don't let Holloway come out here," she called in a hoarse half-whisper.

Parker's frown deepened as he shut the door and came toward her. "What is it?"

"Memories of Paris." She pointed to the bloody lump on the ground.

He stopped short as he reached the spot. His jaw went tight. "Dear Lord."

She waved toward the dumpster. "Give me a leg up."

They moved to the side of the container and Miranda put a foot on one of the fork pockets. Parker remained grimly silent as he hoisted her up.

Holding her breath, she raised the dumpster lid and did a sweep of the inside with her flashlight. More debris on the bottom, but the container looked basically empty. She let herself take a sniff. No telltale dead body smell, though the odor wasn't good.

She let the lid go and climbed down.

Before she could decide what to do next, Erskine and another officer came around the side of the building.

"Have you found anything?"

"You'll want to see this, Hosea," Parker said.

Erskine hurried over and stopped at the small mound. He blinked just once. His lips went back and forth for a moment.

Finally, he spoke in a dark quiet voice. "Dear God."

The officer with Erskine bent down to study the appendage with his flashlight. "The bone is exposed, the skin pale. Subungual hematoma under the nail." He rose and turned to the dumpster. "Anything in there?"

"We didn't see anything," Miranda told him. "Not much in there. It doesn't look deep enough to cover a body."

With a nod Erskine took out his cell. "I'll get a CSI team over here to confirm that and take care of this—appendage."

Just as he was dialing, Holloway appeared in the back door of the furniture store.

"What's going on?" he called.

"Get back, Holloway," Miranda barked at him.

Ignoring her, he rushed forward. "Why? What is it?"

"Holloway, I said get back in there. Have you finished with that last store?"

He brushed past her and looked down at the spot where everyone was gathered. The glimmer of the wall lights reflected sudden moisture in his eyes.

He put a hand to his head. "Oh, dear God. No. No. No."

"Holloway." Miranda touched his arm.

He brushed her off and stepped back, shaking his head. "No, no, no," he said again. Then he turned and ran back through the door.

"Holloway." She started after him.

Parker reached out for her. "Let him go, Miranda. Give him some space just now."

She stopped. Parker was right. She wouldn't be much comfort to him now. Nothing would.

Erskine hung up. "The team will be here in a few minutes. We'll take over from here and analyze this evidence."

It was a dismissive remark, but Miranda knew there was no use offering the Parker Agency Lab. Not for this.

"Is there anything else we can do, Lieutenant?" she asked.

"You can help us sort through the three hundred bogus leads coming in from the Crime Stoppers line."

Her head went back. Phone work? While the mystery man named Drew and a mangled or possibly dead Audrey Wilson was out there somewhere? And she had a distraught, grieving detective on her hands?

On the other hand, what else was there to do? Becker hadn't turned up any more leads. They were at a standstill.

She turned to Parker. "What do you think?"

Parker gave Erskine a hard steady look. "I can spare some of my staff for that, Hosea. We'll get started tomorrow."

"Okay. Agreed."

Parker turned to her. "Why don't you go find Detective Holloway. I need a moment to speak to the Lieutenant."

"All right. Okay." Wondering what that was about, she gave him a long look, then turned and trotted to the furniture store door.

Parker put his hands in his pockets and stared after his wife. Then he gazed down the back alleyway of the shopping center all the way to the end.

"Our suspects couldn't have been here long," he said, uttering his thoughts aloud.

Following his gaze, Hosea came up beside him. "I take it you didn't find any sign of activity other than this appendage?"

"We did not."

So Drew and Audrey were holed up somewhere else. Could be nearby. Could be miles away. But they'd been here in Atlanta this morning. That was certain.

Parker turned to Hosea. "I want to apologize for my detective's behavior."

Erskine seemed surprised at the comment, but not angry. "It's understandable. Apparently he was close to his ex."

"I'm afraid so. I want you to know we'll keep him in check."

He nodded. "Seems like Steele's the one who's handling him."

Parker wasn't going to divulge what an ordeal she thought she had on her hands. "I've formed a special unit at the Agency. Miranda's in charge of it."

"I see."

Hosea didn't seem surprised. After long years of working together, Parker felt he could read the man fairly well. They were once on the force together. Hosea had never quite forgiven him for leaving the APD to go out on his own, no matter how much he'd been able to help with cases over the years. Parker wanted a smoother relationship with him for Miranda.

"We haven't always seen eye-to-eye in the past."

"No. You don't always play by the rules, Parker."

"And you always do. Nonetheless, I want you to know I've always respected you."

Brows rising, Erskine let out a long slow breath. But he dodged the remark. "Your wife has come a long way since she first came to Atlanta."

That was good to hear. Parker allowed himself a wry smile. "From a jail cell to head of an investigative team. I'm very proud of her."

"You should be. That incident in Jasper County—that took a lot of guts."

He was glad Hosea saw the courage in what she'd done, but he could never know the depth of it. Or of his own gratitude. She'd risked her own life, her own sanity to save his daughter that day.

"She has that in spades," Parker agreed.

"Apparently."

"I'm glad to hear you think so. I hope you'll give her your cooperation in the future."

Coming back to himself, Erskine stuck out his chin. "About as much as I give it to you."

Parker gave him a pat on the shoulder. "I'll take what I can get, Hosea."

CHAPTER TWENTY-ONE

As soon as she stepped out of the front door of the furniture store, Miranda could hear the heartrending cries.

She found Holloway on a weathered iron bench, his head in his hands, sobbing. Her heart going out to him, she sat down beside him and waited.

After a long moment, he raised his head and stared out across the parking lot at the lone CSI truck that had arrived a few minutes ago.

"He's going to kill her," he said in a hoarse whisper filled with despair. "I know he is."

She might be dead already, but that was the last thing Miranda could tell him. Instead she said, "Erskine and his team are going to handle the investigation on the evidence. They'll find something."

"It'll be too late."

"You don't know that."

"I can't stand thinking about it, but it's all I can think about. That guy. What is he doing to her? What's she feeling? What's she going through? I should be there. I should be rescuing her."

No, that wasn't his place anymore. It hadn't been for three years. "You'll drive yourself crazy with thoughts like that."

"I can't help it, Steele. I just can't help it."

He stared out into the darkness again, rocking himself. With his disheveled hair and suit coat, he looked ten times worse than he had in Austin. His eyes were red and swollen. He was going on fumes.

Miranda didn't know what to do. She couldn't offer any comfort. There wasn't any to give.

At last she dared to lay a gentle hand on his back. "You need rest."

"I can't—"

"You won't be any good to this investigation if you're exhausted, Holloway."

He kept shaking his head.

She glanced toward the end of the building and saw Parker coming around the corner with Erskine and a few of the other officers.

As the police moved to the truck, he started toward her and Holloway.

She got to her feet. "C'mon. We'll take you home. Drink a beer or two. And don't come in until ten tomorrow."

Unable to find a reply to that, Holloway rose and followed them out to the Mazda.

It was late, but they found a Chinese takeout place, and Parker bought a mound of food for everyone. Then they dropped Holloway off at his apartment with a sack of chow mein and crab rangoons. Watching him drag himself up the steps to his door, Miranda hoped he would eat some of it. And take her advice and get some sleep.

Parker drove back to the penthouse, and half an hour later they were sitting at the counter of its gleaming kitchen eating what they could of the take-out.

"We'll have to keep Curt distracted tomorrow," Parker said, scooping pieces of chicken onto Miranda's plate.

She took a bite and chewed thoughtfully. "Sorting through those messages will do it. Most will be bogus, no doubt."

"Yes."

She only hoped Holloway wouldn't make something out of nothing and go off on his own again.

She pushed the noodles around on her plate with her fork.

"Let the frustration go for tonight." Parker's low voice soothed her like a warm bath.

And yet, as she finished her food her mind kept racing with the details. The obituary in the Georgetown paper. The security photo at the airport. And now this—mutilation. What was the point of it?

"I don't know, Parker. It doesn't add up. Something isn't right. It feels like—"

He reached for her plate. "Like we're being jerked around?"

She almost smiled at how he'd uttered her very thought. "Yeah. That's exactly what it feels like."

He put the dishes in the sink and reached for her hand. "We'll figure it out tomorrow."

He was right. It was all they could do. Let it go for tonight. But just as she slid off her stool, her phone buzzed.

"What is it?" Parker asked, concerned.

She looked at her screen and her back went stiff. "A text from Becker." She read it to him. *"Got a hit on the guy from facial recognition. Real bad dude."*

She tapped the link he'd sent and the attached report opened. The first thing she saw was a set of mean dark eyes staring at her. A mug shot from Los Angeles County where he'd been arrested two years ago—at the age of twenty-four.

His name was Drew Iwasaki.

She recognized the choppy black hair hanging nearly to his shoulders, the expressive dark brows, the chiseled face full of mockery, as if he were thinking, "You assholes can't hold me."

According to the report, Iwasaki had been arrested a bunch of times, but never convicted. He was suspected of running with a Japanese gang in LA, involved in the usual stuff. Extortion, prostitution, drug smuggling.

"Never convicted," Parker read over her shoulder.

Her stomach tightened. "He's connected."

"Most probably."

But to who or what? No way to find out tonight.

"We'll pick this up tomorrow," Parker said.

He was right. They couldn't do anything with the information tonight. She sent Becker a "good job" text and stuffed the phone back in her pocket.

They stuffed the leftovers in the fridge, the trash in the compactor, and made their way upstairs.

A hot shower made her feel better physically, but did nothing for her heart. As she crawled into bed and snuggled up against Parker's strong shoulder, the echo of Holloway's cries came back to her.

She closed her eyes, trying to shut them out, but her mind kept asking the inevitable questions.

Where was Audrey Wilson? Was she still alive? And if so, what condition was she in? And most of all—how would they ever find her?

CHAPTER TWENTY-TWO

Drew Iwasaki stepped through the door at the end of the creepy cave-like hall in the underground labyrinth.

He cantered down the ramp, and cradling two cold bottles of hard cider in the arm of his leather jacket, he pressed the button on the control panel that opened the heavy iron entrance to the lab. When it slid open, he trotted down the second ramp with a spring in his step.

Feeling his skin start to cool at the lower temperature, he stopped to eye the huge vents running up the concrete walls that pumped in sanitized air from outside. Overhead the thirty-foot high ceiling was a tangle of humming shafts for heating and cooling, electricity from the generators, and water pumped in from the nearby creek. Huge fluorescent lights illuminated the massive thousand-square-foot space. Dug five hundred feet into underground rock, it had taken two years to build this fortress.

All for him. Well, mostly.

Still, this was power. He couldn't believe he was here. The thought made him giggle.

There were plans to add on to the fortress, as well as promises to provide minions for getting supplies and cleaning up. But they had to prove themselves first.

A metal framework along the walls held cages with some of the experiments. In one of the cages, rats were greedily gorging themselves on insects until they burst. In another, a white rabbit with electrodes attached to its ears jumped every time a shock was administered at automatic intervals.

His favorite had been the gerbil they'd gotten to run backwards on the exercise wheel. It would run and run and run, never stopping to eat or drink or even catch its breath. An iconic picture of the rat race of modern society, his great-uncle would say. Run and run and run. Until it died and fell off. And then they'd get another one. They'd been through half a dozen gerbils now, each one lasting a little longer. The record now was eight days on the wheel.

But in the center of the room was the chair.

The chair had surpassed the gerbils in entertainment value now that they'd advanced to human experiments. Long and narrow and uncomfortable, the chair had tight leather straps to hold them down and a nest of electrodes to hook to their heads while the testing and conditioning was done.

So far, he'd been stunned by the results. Of course, those results didn't last without the Elixir—Drew's word for the homemade brew that was key to it all. But they had plenty of that.

His gaze moved to the long L-shaped counter. There he was, Phineas Lee Bach, his so-called partner. This place was his brainchild, or so he claimed. But Drew thought of him as his bitch. A minion he needed to advance his status in his great-uncle's eyes.

Phineas was the creator of the Elixir.

Smug and presumptuous as always, he balanced his skinny frame on a stool while he hunched over a microscope.

Buds in his ears that made him oblivious to his surroundings, he paused occasionally to peck at a laptop. He always wore that pressed white lab coat over a wrinkled T-shirt and torn jeans. Trying to make himself look important. But his sandy sheepdog-like hair, his thick glasses, and his acne sprinkled face betrayed the fact he'd just turned eighteen.

Boy genius, they called him. Hah. He was just a kid.

Drew strolled over and set one of the hard cider bottles next to the laptop.

Phineas started at the movement and glared at Drew as he pulled out his ear buds. "I told you not to sneak up on me."

"I'm giving you a reward. It's late, and you've been down here for hours."

His knobby nose wrinkled in disapproval as he slid the bottle away. "How's your cougar?" he sneered in his adolescent voice.

Drew scoffed. "She's only five years older than me."

"She's still out of your league. She'd never have fallen for you without my help."

Without the Elixir, he meant. "What do you mean? It was because she fell for me that I was able to shoot her with your magic perfume. You know women can't resist me."

On their first date in Austin, a small spray of the Elixir had made her open up and tell him all he needed to know about her ex. In particular, that she was still in touch with him and had his phone number.

That was when he'd come up with the idea of the bank robbery.

Chuckling, Drew slid onto the stool across from the kid and opened his bottle. "And the side benefit is your brew makes her fuck like a rabbit. She wore me out just now."

Phineas rolled his eyes. The horny adolescent was jealous.

"Is she locked securely in her room?" he said.

"Of course, she is."

"You made sure?"

"Yes, Phin. I made sure."

No one could escape the ten-by-twelve windowless chambers with the twelve-foot-thick concrete walls they'd had built for their experiments. Plus, the catacomb of passageways throughout the place were equipped with enough horrifying booby traps to prevent escape. He and Phineas had designed them together and overseen them while they were being built.

So what was he worried about?

"And you've been taking the antidote?"

"Two drops under the tongue twice a day. Just like you said. I don't want to end up with zombie brain." He chuckled at his own joke, glad Phin knew what he was doing when it came to chemicals.

Phineas didn't laugh. The young man released the microscope clips and removed the specimen he'd been working on with a pair of tweezers. A moth whose nerve endings he'd been probing. He dropped it onto the counter to study its twitching a moment. Then reached for a tissue, crushed it, and wiped its contents into the trash.

His lips twisted in a serious scowl, he returned to his laptop. "I told you we couldn't screw this up, Drew."

Laughing again, Drew took a deep satisfying swallow of his drink. "You think too much."

Drew got up and moved over to the gerbil cage. The furry brown-and-white creature inside was still running. Its little brown eyes had a look of desperation. Kind of like the look in Experiment One's eyes when he'd hacked off her toe.

The wheel rattled to a stop and the gerbil fell to the bottom of the cage with a small thud.

He laughed at the thrill the sight gave him. "Number Eight is done."

Phineas pecked at the laptop keys. "Noted," he said with his usual indifference.

Beer in hand, Drew strolled around the room studying the cages.

There was a time when neither of them had thought much. Not beyond the next fish they would catch or the next ballgame they'd play. It hadn't been so long ago that they'd been running around the fields of the commune where they'd been raised.

Drew had been eight when Phineas came along. His mother had died giving birth to him, and Phineas was given to one of the concubines to nurse. Drew had been sad when they told him Mary Ann was gone. He had no idea where his own parents were, and Phineas's mother had taken care of him. She'd fed him, told him stories, and sung him songs. Those songs had always seemed to have some hidden meaning behind them. He'd come to believe it was about his destiny, and the power that would be his someday. And so he'd had taken a liking to the little kid who was Mary Ann's orphan. He was curious, smart, entertaining. What was more, he was the grandson of the commune's powerful leader, Lee Bach.

But as soon as Phineas could talk—which had been early—his grandfather had taken him under his wing for training.

Lee Bach had worked for the government on a secret mind control program in the seventies. Enraged when the program was shut down, Bach had formed the commune in central Kentucky with a handful of followers including Drew's great-uncle, Katsu Iwasaki.

Over the past three decades, Lee Bach had developed the place into a thriving community where he could carry on his work. And although on the outside the commune appeared to be a group of idealistic society dropouts, in reality they were not into peace or mutual respect or the environment.

They were into power, influence, manipulation.

And of course, money. They lived simply on the outside, but the leaders had bank accounts with balances in the millions. From a simple hut, Drew's great-uncle Katsu had managed the criminal movements of Asian gangs across the country for years. When he was fifteen, Drew had left the commune to make a name for himself among those gangs. Until he was recruited for this new assignment.

His great-uncle told him of the underground lab near Atlanta that had been under construction for two years and had just been finished. Lee Bach had insisted Phineas be put in charge of the project, and great-uncle Katsu had arranged for Drew to be his partner. But Drew aimed to take control. He knew neither Lee Bach nor great-uncle Katsu had commissioned the structure. And the funds to build it hadn't come from the commune.

It came from someone great-uncle Katsu referred to only as "Our Benefactor." Someone higher up. Drew was going to show this person what he was made of.

He slid back onto his stool. "You don't want the drink I brought you?"

"Alcohol dulls the brain." Phineas snatched his bottle off the counter and went to the fridge to put it away. He closed the door with a slam. He didn't think it was time to celebrate. "Somebody's got to do the thinking around here."

"We both do plenty of that."

"Are you crazy? This was our first real assignment. Our first proof-of-concept. Our Benefactor wanted this operation to be carried out discreetly. No undue attention. No fanfare of any kind. It was supposed to look like an accident. Now you're on the news and those two detectives are after us. Plus the whole APD."

So that was what he was upset about. Drew took a swallow of beer. "It's not that bad."

"Not that bad?" Phineas screeched. "Have you read the files we were sent? These people aren't pushovers."

"Yes, I read the files." He knew about more than just the detective he was supposed to target. "I know Wade Parker is supposed to be the sharpest PI in the southeast. And Miranda Steele has faced down a slew of psychotic killers. But she has a weak spot. Her ex husband."

"She killed him."

"And she's seeing a therapist because of it."

Stubbornly Phineas shook his head. "All you were supposed to do was get the girl to call her ex, and when he showed up at the bank, get her to shoot him dead. Then disappear. No media coverage. No other detectives. No freaking car chase."

"Steele and Parker were supposed to be on vacation. I made sure of that. I called the office and pretended to be a client. The receptionist told me the investigators wouldn't be available for another week. I don't know how they got there, but it didn't matter. They couldn't stop us." He couldn't help cackling over it. "You should have been there at the bank."

Phineas stared at him a long moment, then slid his arms on the counter and leaned forward with a geeky grin. "Did she really try to shoot him?"

Drew nodded with pride. "Right after I gave her the signal behind the knee. And used the Elixir."

"I knew it would work. All due to the precise management of dopamine and serotonin levels plus specialized conditioning techniques."

Drew snickered. "And when we were driving away in the van, all I had to do was give her a command, and she went to the back and tossed out that spike strip I brought along. It was heavy, but she managed it. You should have seen those cops and what it did to that Lamborghini."

"I did see it. It's on the news." Phineas pointed to his laptop.

"That was the easy part. I still can't believe she got the detective to show up at the bank in the first place."

"He's a rescuer type," Phineas's voice took on that expert tone of his. "Ex-Marine and all. And he's remained unmarried after their divorce. Statistics show sixty-four percent of males who remain unattached after a break-up still have feelings for their former wives."

Statistics. "Yeah, but next time we'll need to give our experiment some target practice. She missed by a mile."

Phineas grew quiet. Drew could see fear on his pimply face.

He shook his head. "You made a mess of it. And then you go to the airport and get yourself and the girl caught on the security camera?"

"That was part of my plan."

Phineas shook his hands in the air. "And that obituary in the Georgetown paper? What were you thinking?"

Drew lifted a finger from his beer bottle. "Thinking ahead."

Phineas just stared at him.

"It was a red herring. Meant to misdirect, confuse. Get it?" For a genius he sure could be dense sometimes.

"Like the photo at the airport?" Phineas sneered.

"The photo I let them get of me and the girl. It worked. It got the detectives off our trail. They went straight off to Austin, just like I said they would."

"But now they're back."

"Following my lead." He had to chuckle again at his own cleverness. He'd show his great-uncle who the genius here was. "By the way, Experiment One is gone."

"The girl you picked up on the street? What do you mean, she's gone?"

Drew shrugged. "She bled out after the toe thing."

He chuckled to himself as he remembered her trying to hack off her own toe with a steak knife after a session in the chair. Drew had made her think she was giving herself a pedicure. Damn, he was good.

Of course, she passed out before she finished. He'd whacked off the rest with his pocket knife, then put it in a bag and hidden it in his jacket for his own use later. That was even more brilliant. He wondered what kind of circles the police and the detectives were running around in now.

Phineas slammed his palm down on the counter. "I cauterized it myself."

He was worried about losing her? He raised his palms. "Didn't work."

"You didn't watch her?"

"I was too busy with Experiment Two." He waggled his brows. The detective's ex was a hot one under the influence of the Elixir.

"And now we have a dead body to dispose of?"

"You'll think of something."

"No, you have to think of something. You have to fix this, Drew."

He chuckled. "I'm having too much fun."

"What if that toe leads them to us? What if they find us?"

"Never happen."

"And I don't have to tell you what will happen if Our Benefactor doesn't get what he wants. He'll shut down this facility. My dream. My life's work."

"Life's work? You're a kid."

Phineas began to mutter to himself. "Because of my grandfather, he'll probably spare me, but it won't be that way for you."

His smile gone, Drew put down his bottle and glared through Phineas's thick glasses. Why wasn't he listening? He'd already worked it all out.

"Don't worry, Phin. We're going to Plan B."

"Plan B?" Phin's thin brows shot up over his glasses. "What do you mean by that? You're not going to let her out again, are you? She's wanted by the police."

Smirking to himself Drew finished his beer, sauntered over to a nearby trashcan, tossed the bottle in. "I'm going to let her go back to work."

"To the movie set?"

"Don't worry. The producer will keep an eye on her. My guys have been supplying him with recreational drugs for years. He owes me."

"Drew—"

"I've got it all worked out. This time, we're going to get that ex-Marine. Just listen." And he slid back onto the stool and began to explain everything.

CHAPTER TWENTY-THREE

The next day was a downer.

Miranda dragged herself into the office that morning to discover Parker had brought in a small team of background checkers and bodyguards to work for OT on Sunday. They were set up in the main cube area, already busy on their laptops and phones. Miranda recognized Bill Taylor and Amir Khan from her IIT class. She didn't know the others.

Hoping Parker didn't want her to take charge of them, too, she zipped down the aisle and headed for the lab. There she found Holloway and Becker hunched over their laptops.

From the look on Holloway's face Becker hadn't shared the intel he'd learned about Drew Iwasaki last night.

She was grateful for that.

The smell of strong coffee made her mouth water. Turning her head she saw another round of bagels spread out along the counter. Apparently Becker had brought enough for everyone. The new team had devoured the fare, leaving crumbs and empty boxes and open containers of cream cheese in their wake.

Miranda glanced at the time on her phone. Nine-forty-five. She put a hand on her hip and turned to Holloway. "You weren't supposed to come in until ten."

"I slept as long as I could, Steele," he said without looking up from his screen.

He did look a little better. His clothes were fresh and his hair was combed. But dark circles lingered under his eyes.

Beside him Becker looked concerned, but he didn't say anything.

"Anything promising yet?" she asked.

"Not really."

Giving up on conversation, Miranda got her laptop and set up next to the bagels on the counter. She began by reviewing the progress the others had made, going through the transcripts from calls coming in to the police from the public.

It was hours of tedious work that led nowhere. One caller was convinced the mystery man in the photo on the news was her ex-boyfriend, but one of the bodyguards had called her mother and discovered the boyfriend was Irish and had red hair. Not even a vague match.

A dozen people said they had seen the couple getting out of the white van and running across a field together. Most of them mentioned a location different from where the van had actually been found. Nobody could say where the couple had gone. One guy said the woman in the photo of Audrey was his ex-wife. An old lady insisted she was her daughter, a woman one of the background checkers confirmed had passed away a year ago.

The time ticked by. Parker had sandwiches brought in for lunch, and Miranda ate hers alone in her office, letting the others enjoy a few moments of camaraderie with their peers. She used to be one of them and she missed it. Lonely at the top.

But it was Audrey Wilson's situation that consumed her thoughts. They were getting nowhere, and time might be running out for Holloway's ex. The guy in black named Drew Iwasaki might be hacking her to pieces at this very moment and there was nothing she could do about it.

At the unpleasant thought, she put her sandwich away and got back to work.

The afternoon dragged on with little progress. Shortly before six, Erskine called and asked for her.

Surprised he didn't want to speak to Parker, she took the call.

He told her his people had traced the print from the toe she'd found yesterday to hospital records at Grady. The victim's name was Rebecca Duncan, born twenty-six years ago. After more investigation, they discovered Rebecca Duncan was homeless and had no living relatives. As far as Erskine's officers could ascertain, she'd been living under the Jackson Street Bridge for the last two years. They were interviewing the street people there to find out if anyone had seen the man in the police photos named Drew.

Good luck with that.

Jackson Street Bridge. While Erskine filled her in on more details, she took her phone and did a search. South of the Old Fourth Ward. About three miles from the shopping center.

Didn't tell them much.

Miranda told the lieutenant what Becker had discovered about the man named Drew Iwasaki last night and said she'd forward the information to him.

Erskine thanked her and hung up.

Homeless girl. Twenty-six. Probably an addict. The gangbanger Drew Iwasaki had picked her up off the street and done God-knows-what with her. They might find a body soon.

She didn't know what she'd do with Holloway then.

She went back to her laptop in the lab and worked for a few more hours. Just when she could take no more, Becker's phone beeped.

He jumped and the phone slid to the floor.

"Sorry," he said, scooping it up. "Text," he explained.

He must be talking to Fanuzzi. Holloway had gone down the hall for a break a few minutes ago.

Suddenly Becker leapt from his chair. "Oh my gosh. Look at this, Steele." He held the phone out to her. It wasn't from Fanuzzi.

She read the text and frowned. "Meg Ryan."

Hopping from foot to foot, Becker began to scroll through the conversation he'd been having. "After what you learned in Austin yesterday, I resent my requests to the local movie production companies, telling them the person we were looking for started last week and might be using a different name."

"Different name?"

"I thought if she wanted folks to think she was dead she might be using an alias."

"That was smart."

"Thanks. Anyway, this company replied. We found her. We found Meg Ryan."

Confused, Miranda scratched at her hair. "Meg Ryan? Is she playing the lead in Audrey's movie?" And was Audrey really in a movie?

Becker shook his head. "Audrey's going under the name of Meg Ryan."

Miranda recalled Kenisha Trevino said they used to watch Meg Ryan movies together. Audrey loved the actress. But taking her name?

"How can she do that?"

"It's a stage name or something. She only used it for initial registration, not for payroll or anything official. Apparently it's a trick extras use to get noticed. The studio gets their extras from Ad-Lib Casting. They cross-referenced the registration list of new hires from Ad-Lib with their payroll and got a match. Here." He handed her the phone again.

Now she took the time to read the entire conversation.

Apparently Audrey Agnes Wilson had been registered with Ad-Lib Casting under the name Meg Ryan, and was hired out as a non-union extra to Film Mania Studios last Tuesday for their current project.

Miranda wrinkled her nose. "*Echoes of the Dead*? A horror movie?" She might have known that was the type of job Audrey would have landed.

"That's the working title. It's a zombie movie."

"Like that TV show they film here?"

"No. This is something else. It's a made-for-TV thing."

She read the short description. Something about a young boy waking up in a post-apocalyptic world and having to fight off hordes of the undead to survive. Original. She squinted at the name. "Who's Taylor Anthony Jones?"

"The fifteen-year-old star. The latest heart-throb. Callie's crazy about him."

"Really?" In her opinion, Fanuzzi's daughter was too young to be swooning over boys. She returned to the text and read the most important information. "Audrey's got a six a.m. call time tomorrow morning. Is she going to be there?" How could she if she were being held by a crazy toe-hacker?

Becker raised his palms. "Only one way to find out."

Right. She highlighted the text messages and forwarded them to her own phone.

Bright and early tomorrow morning, she and Parker would be there. Might be best not to let Erskine in on this just yet. A police presence would spook Audrey for sure and they'd just have another chase on their hands.

And then there was that other issue.

Craning her neck, Miranda peered through the door and down the hall. No one in sight.

"Becker, can you keep this between us for now?"

"You mean you don't want Curt to know?"

"I don't think he can handle it. You didn't tell him what you found on Drew Iwasaki last night did you?"

Becker shook his head. "No. I was waiting for you to make that call."

"Good." If Holloway knew about Iwasaki's gang background, he'd have a breakdown. "It'll be better if Parker and I confront our fugitive tomorrow. I'll keep you posted."

"Sure, thing. Whatever you say, Steele."

She still didn't like being in charge, but she appreciated that Becker wasn't the type to make waves. He, at least, was loyal. "Promise me you won't say anything to Holloway."

Nodding, Becker did a key-locking gesture on the side of his mouth. "Mum's the word."

"Thanks."

CHAPTER TWENTY-FOUR

Curt Holloway unlocked the door to his one-bedroom apartment and stepped inside. He hadn't wanted to go home yet tonight, but Steele had forced him out of the office at eight and there was nothing else to do.

He stood in the middle of his living room, his mind a blank.

Dirty clothes were strewn across the back of the couch. Unwashed dishes sat in the sink of his kitchen. His trashcans needed emptying.

He was falling apart.

He laughed softly to himself. Audrey would have had a fit if she could see this place. She'd always fussed at him when he left things lying around. His time in the Marines had made him perpetually neat, but every once in a while he'd lapse. No lapsing allowed in Audrey's world.

He remembered getting into a shouting match with her about it once. Actually, several times.

He went into the bedroom hung up his coat and changed into sweats and a T-shirt. He got the laundry basket and went back into the living room to pick up his clothes.

Sudden pain engulfed his heart. He dropped the basket and sank down onto the couch. Where was she? Where was his wife? What was that guy named Drew doing to her?

Steele had told him the director at the Civic in Austin and given her the guy's first name. If he knew his last name, he'd be searching for him in the crime databases.

He couldn't stop his thoughts. And the investigation was almost at a standstill. He knew Steele had kept him busy with office work to keep him distracted today. If only somebody had gotten a lead.

He felt so helpless.

At least Mr. Parker had told him what Erskine had learned. The toe Steele found yesterday at the shopping mall wasn't Audrey's. That was some comfort. But it had belonged to some homeless girl. Were they both being held by this Drew character?

Steele said there would be more calls to go through tomorrow. He didn't want to go through calls. He wanted to find Audrey.

She was somewhere in Atlanta, but Atlanta was a big place.

Keep busy. Maybe Steele was right. He got up and picked up the basket again.

But what if this investigation dragged on and went cold? What if they never found her?

He was about to take the basket down to the laundry room when his cell buzzed. He dropped the clothes and pulled it out of his pocket.

It was a text from Gen. *We have to talk.*

Yeah, they did. But he didn't know what to say. Gen didn't get what he was going through, and there was no way he could make her. He couldn't deal with her right now.

He was shoving the phone back into his pocket when it rang. Let it go to voicemail, he thought. But he glanced at the number.

He didn't recognize it. He decided to answer.

"Hello?" he said cautiously.

"Hey, hon." Her voice seemed to flood the whole room.

A stab of pain shot through Holloway's chest.

It was Audrey.

His mind raced as his training came back to him. Low key. Don't upset her. Don't let on what you know.

"Hey, baby. What's going on?"

"Oh, Curt. Did I tell you I was in a movie?" Her voice sounded strange. As if she didn't really know what she was doing. Was that guy holding a gun on her? Play along.

"A movie? Really? You got a part in a movie?"

"We're shooting tomorrow morning. I have a six a.m. call time. They said I can have a guest. I'd love for you to come by and watch. I want to talk to you."

"Talk?" He wanted to ask if she was okay. He wanted to find out where she was. But he was afraid she'd hang up if he did.

"We have so much to catch up on, don't you think so?"

"Oh, yes. Yes, we do."

"Can you meet me there?"

"At the set? Where is it?"

"Bellwood Quarry." She gave him the directions and told him where she'd be. He rushed for a piece of paper and scribbled it all down.

"I'll be there. Can't wait to see you."

"Me, too. See you then." The phone went dead.

Kicking the laundry basket aside, Holloway went to his bedroom and took out his holster, his clips, and his 9mm Sig, the weapon the Agency had issued to him. Sitting down at his desk he unlocked the slide, unloaded, gave the chamber a check. Methodically he began to disassemble the gun. Slide, recoil spring, barrel. He wiped each piece off with a cloth, then brushed them, checking each piece carefully.

He was going to make sure his weapon was clean and loaded. He was going to be ready.

If Audrey really showed up at that movie set with that guy named Drew tomorrow, he was going to make sure he'd get her away from him.

And maybe take care of that creep in the process.

CHAPTER TWENTY-FIVE

The tall grass brushed against her bare shins as she strolled through the field in her gauzy white dress. She moved slowly, relishing each step as if it was the first she'd ever taken. The air smelled sweet. As she went along, the grass became higher and the pre-morning dew began to kiss her knees.

Still, she went on. Into the mist.

Into the darkness.

The trees were thick around her now. Their branches bowed down, snatching at her hair. The mist engulfed her. The scent in the air grew stale.

Suddenly she couldn't breathe.

And then she heard a cry from somewhere far away in the distance. A faint echo.

"Help me."

Her heart began to pound with fear. She had to find her. She had to find her now. Before it was too late.

She spun around, but the mist was like whirling waves around her. The broad tree trunks blocked her view.

She heard it again.

"Help me."

"I'm here," she called out. "I'm coming."

But the thick grass twisted around her ankles making it hard to walk. She struggled with each step as the voice rang in her head over and over.

"Help me. Please, help me."

She tried to move faster, but now the grass blades had grown tiny sharp barbs. They dug into her flesh as she went, making her legs sting with pain.

"I'm coming," she called out again.

But she couldn't see anything in front of her now. The mist was too thick.

And then it cleared.

She looked down at her bare feet and legs. They were scratched and bloody. A spiked chain was wrapped around her shins. The chain extended beyond her legs. It lay stretched over the ground like a long rope. She followed the length of it with her gaze and saw it ran all the way over to a tall pine tree. A woman stood at the trunk of the tree, the chain wrapped around her waist.

Her hair was golden and she wore the same gauzy dress. But her eyes were big with fright.

"Help me!" she cried.

She picked up the chain, ignoring the barbs as they pierced her hands, and hurried toward her. The chain grew heavy in her arms, but she kept going. At last she reached her.

"I can get you out," she said, and began to lift the chain from her waist.

The barbs dug into her palms. She kept working the chain, trying to loosen it, disregarding the blood now dripping from her hands.

"No, you can't," the woman said.

"Why not?"

"Because of him."

There was a loud roar behind her. She turned and saw the grill of a white van racing toward her at a furious speed. Its engine growled. It was going to crash into the tree, smashing both her and the woman to bits.

It was almost here!

Miranda sat up and startled awake. Her chest heaved with fear and shock. What was that noise? The van? No. It was a loud, annoying beep, beep, beep coming from the nightstand.

Her phone alarm.

Good grief. She snatched it up and looked at the time. Four-thirty.

With a heavy groan, she lay back and squeezed her eyes shut.

"Good morning."

Reluctantly she opened one eye again and saw Parker standing beside her, fully dressed and holding a steaming cup of something that smelled wonderful.

She wrinkled her nose. "How dare you be so awake and chipper at this hour?"

He chuckled. "One swallow of coffee should cure your bad mood." And then he looked closer and his smile faded. "You had a bad dream."

"Yeah, yeah." She waved it away.

"Miranda."

"We don't have time to deal with it now. I'll make another appointment with Dr. Wingate later."

She didn't want to face the bad feelings that were still clinging to the cobwebs in her head.

She got out of bed and took the cup from his hands. She swallowed a big gulp. "You were right. All better."

He took the cup out of her hands and set it down on the nightstand "We can take a few moments to talk."

She slid her arms around him and buried her face in his strong chest. "All I need is a moment with your arms around me." Closing her eyes she relished the feel of his gentle hands rubbing her back.

The bad feelings evaporated. More Parker magic.

"Mmm," she murmured.

"Mmm," he murmured back, his lips moving temptingly over her hair, and his hands sliding down to her backside, making her skin glow.

Really no time for that. Forcing herself to pull away, she gave him a quick kiss. "I'm fine. We've got to go."

"Yes, you're right," he smiled slyly. "You are in charge, after all."

She waved a finger at him. "And don't you forget it."

CHAPTER TWENTY-SIX

Miranda sat in Parker's Mazda and cursed Atlanta traffic under her breath.

Even though they'd gotten up at four-thirty, they still had to slough through the slow-moving vehicles on I-85 and I-75. Even when they finally made it to the surface streets that they had to take to reach the location of the movie set, they couldn't get much above thirty-five mph. They'd be lucky if they made it before filming started.

And yet the closer they got, the more Miranda thought this was going to be an exercise in futility. If Audrey was being held captive, she wasn't going to show up for her job. And if she was a willing partner with Drew, she wouldn't, either. She'd be afraid someone would spot her and arrest her.

Could Audrey have teamed up with a gang member to kidnap a homeless girl? That was hard to believe, but so was the bank robbery.

Parker cut into her thoughts. "Curt was relieved yesterday when I told him the appendage you found behind the shopping mall wasn't Audrey's."

Miranda took a sip of strong coffee from the travel cup she was grateful Parker had given her. Her earlier dose of caffeine had worn off. "Thanks for handling that for me."

"No problem."

"The two incidents might not even be related."

"A possibility."

Parker liked to leave the options open. But it was pretty strange to get a call from a woman who fired a gun in a bank at the same place a woman's hacked-off toe was left.

"What I still don't get is if Audrey is the victim in this case, what was she doing with a gun in her hands at the bank?"

"Not usually what a kidnapper does with his victim," Parker agreed.

"And why did she toss that spike strip on the road when the police were chasing her? She should have been begging to be rescued."

"Yes."

"And why team up with a guy like Drew Iwasaki if you want to be an actress?"

"She believed he got her a part in this film. Evidently he has some connection to the casting company."

Miranda imagined the gangbanger might be supplying a little cannabis as incentive to getting his way. Maybe he had something incriminating on the head of the company. But why would he do that if he wanted to use Audrey to rob a bank?

And why would Audrey go along so willingly with his plan? Was it some sort of Stockholm Syndrome? And if it was, what sort of mental state would they find her in today? If she showed up.

The idea made her antsy, but she was glad she hadn't asked Holloway to come along. That would be a disaster.

The sun was barely coming up when Parker pulled off the pavement and onto a narrow strip of gravel surrounded by gnarled, spooky looking trees. He stopped at the end of the road.

"This is it?" she asked

"This is the path to the quarry. We'll have to travel to the set on foot."

She peered out at the luminous mist seeping in between the tree trunks. It looked ghostly. Like in the nightmare she'd had. Well, it was almost Halloween.

Parker reached into the glove compartment. "We might need these."

He handed her a pair of pocket-sized binoculars and took one for himself.

"You're right. They might come in handy. I take it you've been on a movie set before?"

Without answering, he gave her a mysterious smile. "It always helps to be prepared."

They got out and found a lighted sign marked "Set" a few yards ahead. They followed it to a "Do Not Mow" sign a little farther on. A few more yards led them to another sign with an arrow pointing toward the set area.

Feeling like Hansel and Gretel, Miranda followed the signs down a winding dirt path along the edge of a wide field.

As they walked, Parker pointed off in the distance. "The excavation site is about a mile that way."

Miranda recalled the photos she'd seen online of the century-old granite quarry when she'd researched the spot yesterday. It was a sweeping vista of curving hundred-foot cliffs that descended to a deep blue-green lake at the bottom.

She had wondered how many kitchen and bathroom countertops had been hewn out of the place over the years. And gravestones.

"The city council is redeveloping the site as a park and a water reservoir," Parker said. "My father's on the advisory committee."

Mr. P was into everything. "Meanwhile, movie producers use it for a cool backdrop."

"Just the spot for a majestic vision of a futuristic world."

"Complete with zombies falling down cliffs," she smirked.

But they wouldn't be filming stunts on the rocks today. The signs pointed toward the surrounding woods.

After trudging up a long hill, at last they reached a row of trailers set up for the stars along the edge of the field. Miranda spotted a group of young girls waiting around the steps of one of them. Probably to catch a glimpse of Taylor Anthony Jones. Shouldn't they be in school?

Beyond the trailers they found a tent where actors were being made-up.

Near the entrance a young woman with her hair in a ponytail stood holding a clipboard. She had a frenzied look.

Miranda pointed in her direction. "Let's try her."

Parker walked up to the woman with his killer smile. "Good morning, ma'am. I'm wondering if you could help us."

"Not unless you know how to apply zombie makeup," the woman said without looking up from her clipboard. "Two of my people called in sick this morning."

"I'm so sorry to hear that."

The low sonorous tone of Parker's sexy southern voice caught her attention. Then she raised her eyes and caught a glimpse of his gorgeous face.

"Ooh," she smiled. "Maybe you should try out for a speaking role. Have you ever acted before?

"Not for remuneration."

"It's never too late to start."

"No, thank you. We're looking for a woman on your staff named Audrey Wilson. Actually she goes by the stage name Meg Ryan."

The woman laughed and shook her head. "Must be an extra."

"That's correct."

She consulted her clipboard. "I'm sorry. The background zombies have already been done."

"Audrey is playing a background zombie?" What a glamour job.

"She's an extra, isn't she?"

"Do you know where we can find her?" Parker asked.

"She'd be over in holding with the others, waiting to be called to the set." She waved toward another tent in the distance.

"Thank you." Parker turned to go.

"Hey," the woman called after him. "If you change your mind, give us a call."

Parker only smiled.

With the sun growing brighter, they followed the leaf strewn path to the tent marked "Holding."

Here a young man with red freckles, large ears and yellow shirt stood, ticking off items on his clipboard.

Miranda decided to take this one. "Excuse me."

He jumped and flapped a hand to his chest. "Oh. You shouldn't walk up on me like that."

"Sorry. Didn't mean to startle you, but we're looking for someone."

He shook his head firmly. "The director is busy. I'm afraid you'll have to come back another time."

"We're looking for one of your extras." She took her phone and scrolled to Audrey's picture. "Is this woman here?"

The young man squinted at it. "Hmm. Maybe. I see so many extras."

Miranda debated telling him she was wanted by the police. No, that would only bring unwanted questions. Besides, it was still hard to believe Audrey would show up here after she'd robbed a bank.

"Oh, wait. Let me see that again?" He leaned closer to Miranda's phone. "Yes. That's—um—"

"Meg Ryan?"

He rolled his eyes. "Yes."

"Is she here?" Really? Miranda peeked under the canopy.

The man checked his clipboard. "No. She's on set. Most of the background extras are. They're about to shoot the forest scene. The director wants to get it done in the daylight. It'll probably take all day."

And he just let her come and go like that? This guy didn't watch the news, did he?

"Thanks." Miranda turned in the direction he had pointed.

"Oh, you can't go over there. You have to wait until they're done."

Pretending not to hear him, she waved and smiled. Then she leaned over to Parker. "If we're lucky we might be able to snag her before they start."

"Or after."

CHAPTER TWENTY-SEVEN

With Parker at her side and a slight wind against her face, Miranda trudged up a steep hill toward a thick clump of trees. As she crossed the rise, she saw people in ragged clothes and muddied faces gathered in a group.

A big group. There must have been a couple of hundred of them. A man stood along one side, addressing them through a bullhorn.

Miranda couldn't hear what he was saying. She craned her neck to study the extras. Men, women, a few teens, an elderly man. All wearing clothes that looked about to fall off of them. The skin on their faces did, too.

Makeup.

She wouldn't recognize her own mother in a costume like that. Although her mother could look pretty scary at times.

"How are we going to find her?" she whispered to Parker.

"Needle in a haystack," he murmured, disgust in his tone.

"Let's split up. Maybe one of us can spot her."

He scanned the field and raised a hand. "Let's meet over there at that trailer in half an hour."

That's all the time he wanted to give it? It was enough for Audrey to spot them and run.

"Okay."

"Be careful."

"I'm always careful," she grinned.

She stepped away from him, circling to the left of the group, breathing in the earthy forest smell mixed with the scent from the actors' makeup and clothes. Under a tall pine, there was a guy in a dark plaid shirt. Next to him stood a woman in a long flowing dress streaked with dried blood. As Miranda made her way around them, the group began to move.

Spreading out, they stumbled through the tall grass and dead leaves, arms waving. One of them began making gurgling sounds.

Behind the group she could see large cameras and boom stands hanging over the crowd.

"You're on channel one," somebody said.

Good grief. They were filming already.

Where the heck was Audrey? Concentrate, she told herself. Female. Average height. Blondish hair. If they hadn't dyed it or put some kind of goop on it.

She struggled to keep her distance as she rustled through the leaves, dry sticks snapping under her feet.

Suddenly the extras began to close in around her. Something exploded in the distance. About two hundred rotting zombies started moving toward her. This was too much.

Pop, pop, pop. Shots smoked along the tree trunk in front of her.

She let out a squeal and turned—right into the horde. To her left came a grrring sound. She turned her head and a zombie came straight at her. There was another pop and the zombie's head exploded. Fake blood hit her in the face.

Dear Lord.

A nearby tree went up in flames.

And then she felt teeth on her arm. One of these bastards was actually biting her! She raised her arm and rammed her elbow into his jaw. It fell off onto the ground.

"Hey," he said in a country drawl. "You weren't supposed to do that."

"Oh, yeah?"

But there wasn't time to argue. Five more were coming after her. Enough with the method acting.

Miranda hurried to the nearest tree, jammed her foot onto a low-hanging branch and hoisted herself up. She climbed until she was out of reach of the crazy actors.

Below her the shouting and grring and popping continued. The air filled with smoke and she could hardly see anything. She climbed higher, trying to get a better view, despairing of ever finding Audrey.

And then she remembered Parker's binoculars. She still had them in her pocket, if they hadn't fallen out. She felt for them. They were still there. She pulled them out and scanned the extras below.

"Cut! Cut!" someone was yelling.

Everyone stopped and looked around confused.

Glad these zombies couldn't climb trees, Miranda scanned the faces. None of them looked like Audrey.

Maybe she could locate Parker. She swept her lens over the perimeter of the group. Didn't see him anywhere. Her heart sinking, she did a second pass and a third.

And then something else caught her attention.

No. It couldn't be.

She focused the binoculars, wiped them on her sleeve, and peered through them again. Sure enough.

Far away along the edge of the set was another row of trailers. Beyond them a grassy hill led to a wide forest stretching toward the west. The last trailer sat off by itself. Beside it stood a woman in the requisite creepy clothing and matted shoulder-length hair.

It was Audrey.

Miranda wouldn't have been so sure if it weren't for the person she was looking at.

Walking toward her with his slight limp, and wearing a dark brown suit over his lanky form was Holloway.

How did he get here?

She stuffed the binoculars back into her pocket, scrambled down the tree, and began pushing her way through the teeming extras.

"Where are you going, young lady?" A man in street clothes called after her. Must have been one of the directors.

She turned and bared her teeth at him. "Back off, bud."

CHAPTER TWENTY-EIGHT

Holloway felt more nervous than the first time he'd asked her out on a date.

Audrey stood alongside the trailer wearing a thigh-length nurse's dress covered with fake blood and dirt. Her pretty blond hair was ratted up to look like it hadn't been combed in a month. A trickle of blood came from one of her eyes.

It distressed him to see her like this. It's a movie, he reminded himself. She's got a part in a movie. She hadn't been lying about that, after all.

Her hands twitched at her sides. She was nervous, too.

First date nerves.

She took a hesitant step toward him. "Hi, Curt."

"Hey, babe. It's good to see you again." Not "again." Why did he say "again"?

She frowned and cocked her head in that cute little way of hers. "We haven't seen each other in three years."

She was in shock, denial. If she'd watched some other woman get her toe hacked off—

"Sorry I'm late."

Her frown deepened, the dark makeup magnifying the lines in her forehead, making her look old. "Curt," she said. "What are you doing here? I'm working."

"You asked me to come."

"No, I didn't." She took another step toward him.

She didn't remember calling him? Was she having amnesia? Was that guy named Drew taking advantage of her because of it? He didn't know. All he knew was he had to get her away from him. Away from this place. Now was the best chance he had. The guy in the black leather jacket was nowhere in sight.

They were alone.

Making his move, he took two steps toward her until he was close enough to touch her. He wanted to, but he didn't.

"Why don't we go for a drive?"

She blinked at him as if he had called her a dirty name. "A drive?"

"Yeah, I've got my car right over there." He gestured across the field.

He'd seen Mr. Parker's silver Mazda parked at the end of the gravel road when he'd come in. He didn't know how Steele had learned where Audrey would be today, but he bet she was here with Mr. Parker. He was fuming she hadn't let him know.

But he wasn't going to let that stop him from his mission.

Suddenly Audrey's head jerked back. She reached into the bloody pocket of her nurse's outfit and pulled out a gun. The same one she'd had in the bank.

He should have noticed the bulge in her pocket but it had been camouflaged by the blood and gunk.

Holding the gun in both hands, she pointed it at his heart. "I'm not going anywhere with you, Curt."

Automatically he raised his hands, but managed a smile. "Hey, take it easy, honey. We don't have to go right now."

"Not now. Not ever. Where's my fifty-thousand dollars?"

The money she'd demanded the other day? Somehow she remembered that. "It's at the bank. Why don't we go get it?"

She blinked several times, and her neck twitched as if she had an itch somewhere. What was wrong with her?

Shaking her head, she stepped back, lowering the gun a little. "Oh, no, Curt. I'm not stupid."

"I didn't say you were." Not stupid. She had lost her mind. Something had happened to her and she'd lost her mind. He didn't know what to do.

"This is your last chance, Curt. I'm done waiting for you to come around."

"Okay, babe. What do you want me to do?"

Her eyes glowered. For a moment she looked like a real zombie. "I want you dead."

She raised the gun again.

Instinct took over. Marine instinct. Parker Agency instinct. He grabbed her wrists and shoved her hands up just as the gun went off with a bam.

The blast rang in his ears, making them buzz, but he could hear shouts in the distance. From the corner of his eye he saw cast members and crew running toward them.

Audrey struggled in his grip. "What do you think you're doing, Curt?"

"I'm saving you."

He wrenched the gun out of her hands and tossed it under the trailer. Then he bent down to pick her up.

She beat him off with her fists. "Leave me alone. Stop it."

Another shot whizzed past his head. For a moment Holloway didn't know where it had come from. Then he saw the man standing at the far end of the trailer holding a pistol. Long scraggily black hair. Black leather jacket and pants. Asian face.

Drew.

He let go of Audrey and reached under his coat for his Sig.

"Don't move, soldier boy," the man in black said.

Holloway pulled Audrey behind him and aimed his gun. "Don't you dare try to hurt her. What have you done to her?"

The man didn't answer. Holloway saw his gaze flick to a spot behind him. The crowd was getting closer.

He was just about to turn and hustle Audrey away when she kicked him in the shin. Hard.

"Ouch. What are you doing?"

"Get away from me." She gave him a shove, and he stumbled.

She ran toward Drew. He fired again, and Holloway barely had enough time to roll under the trailer for cover.

He peered out from beneath the vehicle and watched their feet as they ran through the grass. He became aware of a stinging sensation on his arm. He turned his head and saw red on the sleeve of his coat. Blood. The real stuff this time.

He'd been hit.

But Drew was getting away with Audrey. He had to stop them.

He rolled back out from under the trailer, hurried to the far corner for cover, and fired. Missed.

Still running, Drew fired back over his shoulder.

Holloway ducked behind the trailer. The bullet bounced over in the grass somewhere.

He risked another look. They were running over the top of a hill now and there was too little of Drew's frame for another shot.

He couldn't let them get away.

He left the cover of the trailer and took off after them. They disappeared over the rise.

He ran as fast as he could, cursing the leg he'd injured.

At the top of the hill, he stopped and took aim again. But they were too far away.

Down below cars and jeeps were parked along a thick row of pines. Drew and Audrey climbed into a camouflage-colored Jeep and drove off down a dirt path into the woods.

Holloway stood, his mind whirring, his chest heaving. He had to go after them. He had to get to them. But there was no way he could catch up now.

He turned and saw the crowd of folks had reached the trailer. And at their head was Mr. Parker and Steele.

Now he was in for it.

CHAPTER TWENTY-NINE

With her Beretta drawn, Miranda met Holloway halfway up the hill where she'd finally found him—alone.

"What the hell do you think you're doing?" she yelled at him between gasps for breath as she holstered her gun.

He didn't answer. He was out of breath, too.

She looked him over and saw red coming from the upper sleeve of his coat. He was bleeding. "You've been hit."

She'd felt completely helpless watching the altercation while she'd run toward it at breakneck speed.

"I'm okay." He put away his weapon and waved to the area over the hill behind him. "The guy named Drew drove off with Audrey in a camouflage-colored Jeep just now. We've got to get Erskine. The police have got to set up roadblocks."

Parker came up beside the pair. He was winded as well, his hair was gently mussed, and his expensive suit had lost some of its gleam.

"Unfortunately, Detective," he said in a stern voice, "we have no cell reception here. I've already tried to reach him."

Miranda held up a hand. She wanted answers. "Holloway, how did you get here?"

"I drove," he said condescendingly.

"You know what I mean. How did you know about the movie shoot?"

His jaw jutted out with irritation. "Audrey called me."

"She called you? When?"

"Last night. She asked me to meet her here. How did you and Mr. Parker know about the shoot?"

"Becker got a text from Film Mania Studios yesterday. They confirmed Audrey was on their payroll and said she was scheduled to work today."

Holloway's brown eyes blazed. "And you didn't tell me?"

"Looks like I didn't have to." Softening a bit, she touched his arm. "We need to get that looked at."

He winced a little as he pulled out of her grasp. "I'm fine. Audrey's handgun is under the trailer." He pointed at the spot as if he expected her to go under there and get it.

She glanced at Parker and saw he was none too pleased with Holloway's behavior.

"As I was about to say," Parker said with his famous calm composure, "the director has gone to his trailer to call the police on the landline the studio had installed."

"That's going to take too long, sir."

He was right. They'd already lost them.

Leaving Parker to deal with Holloway for the moment, Miranda sprinted over to the rise where she'd last seen Drew and Audrey. Shielding her eyes, she peered down the hill. Then using her binoculars, she made out a winding gravel road through the dense trees. No sign of a camouflage-colored jeep. No sign of anyone. But that road had to lead to the sparse residential area to the south. Were Drew and Audrey hiding out in one of those houses?

She couldn't say, but it would mean more house-to-house canvassing for Erskine and his officers when they got here.

She pressed a hand to her temple, the rage quelling inside her. How dare that creep Drew shoot her detective? Hadn't he just gotten over an injury? And they'd lost them again. They were right there. Audrey was standing right next to Holloway.

And now she was gone again.

She'd shot at him, too. Like she had at the bank. And she'd lured him here to do it. Why? Did she have a life insurance policy on him? Was she harboring a grudge against him for holding her back on her career? Nothing made sense.

Feeling a headache coming on, Miranda trudged back to the far end of the trailer.

She paced back and forth, plowing through the grassy weeds as she went. Holloway was right. They had to do something. But the director had already called the police. Erskine and his men would show up soon. What else could they do now?

Audrey's gun.

They should let Erskine process it, but she could verify where it was. Maybe it would have some trace evidence that would help them locate the pair.

She squatted down to peer under the trailer. She didn't see the gun. It must be at the other end. She rose again and gazed absently at the grass near her feet as her mind raced. Maybe they could get tire tracks from the Jeep. Tire tracks were unique. Maybe they could track down Drew's whereabouts that way.

As she pondered the idea, a glint of something in the grass caught her eye.

She bent down again to study it.

As she stared, an itchy, tingly sensation went down her spine. It wasn't from the grass. It was a feeling she'd felt too many times before. And this time it was spot on.

Wedged beneath the tall blades of unmown grass lay a small amber colored bottle. She couldn't tell if anything was in it.

Don't touch. Don't touch, the voice in her head seemed to say.

I know that, she thought, rising again. But she did take out her cell to snap a picture of it before she went to look for Parker.

As she rounded the trailer's corner, she saw the zombies had caught up to the action. On the doorsteps of the trailer, someone with a first aid kit was looking at Holloway's arm.

Parker stood at the edge of the throng of worried gray-clad extras who were milling about. He looked like he was trying to calm a man in a loose plaid shirt and jeans with a long ponytail down his back. The man was a head shorter than Parker, but he made up for that by waving his arms over his head.

She caught some of his words. "We've lost the light we needed. This is costing money. What are you going to do about that?"

Must be the director.

Obviously irritated with the man, Parker turned his head and caught her eye.

Reading her face, he frowned. "What is it?"

"I need to show you something."

"Excuse me a moment," he told the man and followed her back around the trailer.

She pointed downward. "What do you think that is?"

He bent down to peer through the blades of grass. "Some sort of bottle."

"Do you think Drew or Audrey might have dropped it here?"

"It's possible. This is where Iwasaki was hiding before he fired his weapon."

Or maybe one of the two hundred extras had dropped the bottle here.

Parker took a plastic glove and bag from his pocket. He always carried detective gear. After pulling on the glove, he carefully lifted the vial and slipped it into the bag.

He rose, still studying it.

The dark amber bottle had an eye dropper and was half full of an inky liquid.

"I can only imagine what might be in here," he said somberly.

A shiver went down Miranda's spine. "Me, too. What do we do with it now?"

Just then the crowd of zombies started to rumble. She peered around the trailer and spied Lieutenant Erskine marching across the field, a uniformed officer on either side.

The director hurried over to Erskine. "I'm so glad you're here, officers. There's been a terrible incident."

"I'll be with you in a moment." Erskine strode right past him and up to them. "Parker. Ms. Steele. What seems to be going on?"

Miranda explained about the shooting.

Erskine wasn't happy. The lines in his face growing deeper, he scowled at the crowd of muddy zombies milling around. They didn't brighten his mood at all. "I wish you would have informed me you were coming here today."

Miranda raised her palms. "Well, you know what they say about hindsight."

With a huff Erskine pointed at the plastic bag Parker was holding. "What's that you have there?"

"We think one of the suspects might have dropped it," Miranda said.

Erskine cocked his head and squinted at it. His tight jaw went back and forth. "It will take a week for our people to analyze that." His offhanded way of asking the Parker Agency to do it.

Parker looked to Miranda. Once again, her call. That meant only one thing. Only one person at the Parker Agency who could do a chemical analysis fast. What choice did she have?

She put her hands on her hips and nodded. "Okay. I'll see if I can call in Fry from vacation."

Then she marched over to the director to ask to use his landline.

CHAPTER THIRTY

Fry wanted concessions.

Triple pay for coming in on short notice and three extra vacation days—even after Miranda explained the situation and that it was Holloway's ex they were trying to save.

She caved, hoping Parker would approve the requests.

But after she hung up, she decided Fry was jealous he hadn't gotten to be on the set of a zombie movie.

The director wanted to get back to work, and Erskine asked for help canvassing the nearby area for the camouflage-colored jeep. Since there was nothing else to do at the office, she used the landline again and called Becker to drive down to the set and pick up the amber bottle in Parker's plastic bag. She certainly wasn't going to ask Holloway to do it.

She wasn't letting him out of her sight.

A production assistant confirmed Audrey had received a paycheck last Friday, but had never cashed it. Erskine's men questioned the extras who were in the same scenes as Audrey, but nobody knew much about the young woman who went by the name Meg Ryan.

Another officer crawled under the trailer to retrieve Audrey's handgun. As he bagged and tagged it, Miranda recognized the pink handle from the bank. That bitch had tried to shoot Holloway twice with that gun. If she wasn't a victim here, Miranda would make sure she paid for that.

Accompanied by a few of Erskine's officers Miranda and Parker walked down the hill and got a closer look at the trail where the camouflage-colored jeep had disappeared. They found tire tracks in the dirt, and Erskine called CSI out again to take photos and impressions. They followed the trail over the rough terrain through the gnarled trees to where it spilled out onto asphalt. Mud streaks on the road contained more tracks from the jeep to collect and analyze. Drew Iwasaki was making this part easy.

Of course, all the evidence in the world wouldn't help if they couldn't find him.

Miranda went back to the Mazda with Parker and drove around to the well-kept tin-roofed country homes and questioned the occupants.

No one had seen anything. The residents knew there was a movie shoot going on so they were used to hearing pops and bangs and zombie noises. The only one who had something to report was an elderly lady they found rocking on a porch across from the dirt road with the tire tracks.

Hours had passed since this morning, and the sun was beginning its descent, turning the sky a myriad of color and casting eerie shadows through the gnarled branches onto the fallen leaves along the pavement.

"They think I'm senile, but I'm not," she told them, rocking back and forth. She stopped a moment and fixed her eye on Miranda. Then she raised a bony finger. "You know, don't you, girlie?"

The remark surprised her. "I'm not sure what you mean, ma'am."

"I can tell. You have the gift."

Miranda swallowed. Was the woman talking about the strange sensations she always had when they were close to a lead on a case? How did she know about that?

The woman pulled a shawl around her and rocked again. "They say I'm crazy, but I know what's what. The end is near. I can feel it. I can hear those creatures out there."

Miranda let out a breath and glanced at Parker. This poor old lady thought the zombies were real.

"Thank you for your time, ma'am." She turned to go.

"Aren't you going to ask me if I saw them?"

Miranda turned back. "Saw who?"

"The man you're looking for. The one in the jeep."

Miranda stared at her. They hadn't mentioned the jeep. Parker had only asked if she'd seen anything unusual.

The woman lifted her skinny finger again. "It came out right there. Right where that dirt path leads into those woods. Oh, those woods are full of strange creatures at night."

"What else did you see?" Parker prompted.

"A man with dark hair was driving. Young man. He had a woman with him. He took off that way. He was driving like the wind." She pointed down the road that led back to the main highway.

That was where the tire tracks had led. "Are you sure?"

"Of course, I'm sure."

"Did you happen to get the tag number?"

The woman shook her head. "No."

It helped confirm what they already knew. Drew and Audrey had fled the area that morning at high speed. They weren't holed up in any of the surrounding houses.

"Thank you for talking to us," Miranda said again, and she started down the porch stairs.

"Missy?" the woman said.

"Yes?"

"Don't you want the photo I took with my cell phone?"

"Cell phone?"

The woman pulled it out of her pocket and began to swipe the screen. "Here it is. Pretty clear shot, if I do say so myself. I used to be a photographer, you know."

Miranda blinked at Parker, then came back up the stairs to get a look.

"May I?" She took the phone and showed it to Parker.

He nodded firmly.

The picture showed the tail of the camouflage-colored jeep racing away down the street. And part of the license plate was as clear as day. PQA52.

Drew didn't bother to remove the plate from this vehicle. He was getting cocky. But at last it was something they could use. If enough people recognized this plate, they might have Drew and Audrey in custody tomorrow.

"Can I send this to my phone?" she asked.

The old woman grinned up at her with a knowing look in her eyes. "Of course, you can. Anything for the girl with the gift."

CHAPTER THIRTY-ONE

Miranda passed the photo with the partial plate on to Erskine, and the lieutenant put out a BOLO and released the information to the news stations.

She was standing on the street next to Parker staring into the forest when Holloway strolled up, his suit coat slung over his shoulder. His upper arm was wrapped in a thick white bandage.

"How are you feeling?" she asked him.

"I'm fine," he scoffed. "It stopped bleeding hours ago. The medic on set confirmed it was superficial. She smeared some antiseptic on it and told me to watch for infection. She even gave me a tetanus shot. Happy?"

Not hardly. Watch for infection and watch his back. Miranda was debating whether to give him some time off when her cell rang.

She dug it out of her pocket. It was Fry. She spoke to him for less than a minute and hung up.

She turned to Parker. "Fry's got results. He didn't want to give them to me over the phone. He wants us back in the lab."

Parker scowled at Fry's attitude, but he nodded. "Let's go."

The three of them headed back to their cars and raced up the interstate to the office.

If racing was the word for fighting through a heavy Monday afternoon rush hour on the interstate. Fumes from the eighteen-wheeler rolling noisily beside the Mazda was making Miranda nauseated. And the F-150 in front of them blocked her view.

She glanced out the window and spotted Holloway's white-and-black Mini Cooper with the red racing stripe two lanes over and three car lengths ahead. "I hope he doesn't beat us there," she murmured under her breath.

She heard Parker exhale audibly.

"Let's try a surface street." He took the exit onto Piedmont and headed north.

Traffic was a little better here, and they whizzed along at forty-five mph.

They passed the bank building where the first shooting had taken place last Friday, and made it back to the office a few minutes later. There weren't many cars outside. It was the end of the work day and most everyone had gone home.

Miranda saw Holloway's Mini Cooper pulling into the lot just as she and Parker slipped through the back entrance.

Ten minutes later, they met Becker in the lab area where the test tubes and microscopes were.

Becker leaned over his laptop. "They're here," he told Fry through a communication screen.

Miranda turned to the sealed room marked "Authorized Personnel Only."

Fry didn't come out of the room.

After another minute passed, she took a step toward the entrance. She was about to pound on it and tell Fry to knock off the dramatics when the door flew open and the lab tech emerged from the decontamination room in a bright yellow hazmat suit.

Suddenly concerned she stared at him. "What was in that bottle, Fry? Are we going to have to lock down the office?"

He removed the headgear and his chocolate brown hair tumbled to his shoulders. She noted his beard had grown an inch since she'd last seen him. He must have given up trimming it during his vacation.

He gave her his usual cynical smirk. "You're lucky you didn't find the real stuff."

"Real stuff? What are you talking about?"

He held up the amber bottle. "This is an antidote."

"Antidote for what?"

"That's what I had to figure out," he said with a self-satisfied smile. "I had to reverse engineer the substance. I performed a microscopic examination, the requisite chromotographical and spectrometry tests. There are a few other substances in the liquid, but it's primarily made of physostigmine."

"Physo-what?"

"Phy-so-stig-mine," he said slowly as if talking to a child. "It's an acetylcholinesterase inhibitor used to treat overdoses of scopolamine."

Miranda dug her palms into her temples. Why couldn't Fry speak English? Then she saw the stunned look on Parker's face.

"Scopolamine?" he said darkly.

Fry nodded. "Yes, sir. As far as I can determine this bottle contains some sort of antidote for it."

Miranda racked her brain for her training on street drugs and came up empty. "Scopolamine? What is that?"

"A hypnotic drug," Fry said. "A substance from plants of the nightshade family. It's rumored to be used in South America by criminals. They give targets a drink laced with the substance, take them to an ATM and get them to empty their bank accounts. The victim wakes up the next day and doesn't remember anything about it."

"So it's a mind-control drug."

"Precisely. But there were a few other substances mixed with this antidote. My guess is the victim would be given some admixture of hallucinogenics along with it. Ingesting it would make the subject highly suggestible. In short, it produces zombie brain."

Holloway looked pale as a ghost. "Are you saying someone who was given that stuff could be made to do anything?"

"That's what I'm saying."

"Are you sure, Fry?" Parker asked.

Fry's shoulders went stiff under the yellow suit. "Per procedure, I tested multiple samples, sir. All results were the same. The substance is definitely toxic, but two or three drops would reverse the effects of the hypnotics, in my opinion. My guess is the kidnapper is using this to protect himself."

From the effects of his own drugs. "But he doesn't have it any more."

Fry lifted a shoulder. "He can probably get more, or he has a stash of it somewhere. That's what I'd do—if I were into that sort of thing."

Miranda reached for the back of a chair to steady herself as her mind reeled with what Fry had said. Zombie brain? Suddenly it all made sense. The shootings at the bank. The spike strips. The attempt to shoot Holloway on the movie set today. Drew Iwasaki was using a mind-control substance on Audrey, while he stayed safe with his antidote.

He'd turned her into a real-life zombie.

Did he get it from some of his gang affiliations? And why was he targeting Audrey? Why did he want her to shoot Holloway? And where did they go from here with this investigation?

Becker stepped over to Fry to get a better look at the amber bottle, though he kept his hands at his side. As he stared at it, his stomach rumbled.

His cheeks reddened. "Sorry. We skipped lunch."

"I'll have dinner brought in," Parker said mostly to break the mood of shock in the room.

Miranda didn't want to eat, but they hadn't had anything since early that morning and she was starting to feel dizzy. It was no good working with hungry detectives, and she had to get her wits about her to figure out what to do with this new information.

Becker cleared his throat. "Can we have pizza, sir? I'd like to bring one home to Joanie and the kids."

He was always so thoughtful.

Parker's kind smile told her he was glad to be reminded of the simple pleasures of family life.

"Of course."

CHAPTER THIRTY-TWO

Erskine was still sending in crime stopper calls, and Parker's auxiliary team was working after hours, so Parker treated them to pizza as well.

They gathered in the break room while Miranda, Becker and Holloway took their food back to the cube area of the lab.

While they munched on pepperoni and Miranda loaded her slice with extra jalapeños, Becker watched the news from the tablet he'd set up on the counter. A serious-looking newswoman gave the report.

"Another incident occurred this morning involving the woman who attempted to rob South Exchange Bank on Friday. This time on the set of *Echoes of the Dead*, a new movie being filmed south of the city." She mentioned the camouflage-colored jeep and read off the partial plate while the screen flashed the photo the lady across the street had taken.

Becker wiped pizza sauce off his face. "Looks like the newshounds have already pounced on the information you found."

Miranda stared at the tablet. Would it help find Audrey? Or just drive the pair deeper into hiding?

"I've been running the partial tag number through the database. No hits yet."

She knew that. Parker had retired to his office to keep an eye on the run, and to leave her in charge of everyone. It was too much to hope that the tag number was registered to Iwasaki. The jeep was likely to have been stolen, but if someone saw Drew and Audrey in it, maybe they could narrow down their location.

Miranda pushed her plate away and started to think out loud. "So we can assume Drew is using a chemical concoction to control Audrey."

"It looks that way to me," Becker said, his mouth full of pizza. He swallowed down a gulp of soda. "This afternoon, I mapped out all the places we know they've been. The local ones."

"Let me see."

Becker wiped his hands on a napkin and went to the counter to fiddle with his tablet. He did some magic swiping, and a map of the area appeared with each location marked with a red dot.

Miranda studied it a moment. The bank in Buckhead. The spot where the van was found in Avondale Estates. The deserted shopping center where they found the homeless girl's toe. The movie set at the quarry.

With some imagination, the dots seemed to form a rough circle. "Maybe he's going to strike again in Buckhead next."

"Here? At the office?" Becker's eyes went round with alarm.

"We'll be ready for him," Holloway said darkly.

Things began to click. She turned to Holloway. "You have the number Audrey used to call you last night, don't you?"

He nodded and pulled out his phone.

"Let me see it." She peered at the number on his screen. "That's not the same phone we traced to the shopping mall."

"They probably change phones every day. This number probably won't work."

"But if it does, we could use it to draw her out again."

Becker didn't like that idea. "If she's under the influence of those drugs, she doesn't know what she's doing."

He was right. It was Iwasaki who was calling the shots.

Becker blew out a breath of irritation. "I still can't believe Drew Iwasaki is using that drug on Audrey. And protecting himself from the effects with the antidote. A twenty-six-year-old gangbanger wouldn't be able to come up with something like that on his own."

Holloway opened his mouth wide and turned to Becker. "Drew—Iwasaki? Twenty-six-year-old gangbanger? How do you know that?"

Becker let out a squeaking sound as he looked at Miranda. "You didn't tell him?"

She hadn't wanted to set him off. Becker had promised not to say anything. Apparently he'd forgotten that.

She turned to Holloway. "Becker found a record on Drew Saturday night. His last name is Iwasaki. He's involved in gang activity and was arrested in Los Angeles County two years ago. He's been arrested several times, but never convicted."

Miranda watched Holloway's chest heave as he took in the information. "And you didn't tell me this?"

"No, I didn't." She didn't have to explain her reasons to him.

He got to his feet and tossed down his napkin. "I need some air."

"Where are you going?"

"Out."

And he stomped out of the lab and slammed the door behind him.

Miranda shut her eyes and shuddered, forcing down the anger. She didn't need this now. If Audrey was a victim of mind-control, if Iwasaki was feeding her drugs to make her shoot at people, they needed to find her fast. But if that were true, that meant Iwasaki wanted Holloway dead. That didn't make any sense at all. Who was this guy?

She turned to Becker. "Have you got any more information on Iwasaki?"

Becker shook his head. "After his last arrest, his record is clean."

"Or someone wiped it for him. He's connected."

"Looks that way."

But to who? Or what?

She got up and began putting away the pizza leftovers.

"Sorry about talking too much," Becker said.

"It's okay," she said wearily. "He'd find out sooner or later and react the same way. Here. You can take these home to Fanuzzi and the kids," she said over her shoulder.

"I don't think that will be anytime soon."

She looked up and saw Becker wasn't next to her. He was standing at the door, peering out at the cubes in the main area. Miranda stepped over to see for herself.

The place was a beehive. Erskine's press release was drawing in a ton of new calls. It was just as well. They needed something to do. And if she put Holloway to work, maybe he'd get over his mad.

"I'd better go find our AWOL investigator."

And she handed Becker the pizza box and stepped past him through the door.

CHAPTER THIRTY-THREE

Feeling like a complete failure as a boss, Miranda went down the hall scanning the aisles and peering into dark offices. She passed the water cooler and the break room without seeing a trace of her errant detective.

If he'd gone home, it might be for the best.

Then she took a turn and spotted light coming from one of the offices. Gen's. Was she still here? And was Holloway in there with her?

The last thing she wanted was to get in the middle of a love spat, but at least she'd know where he was.

Her stomach tightening, she approached the door. She stood outside and listened. No voices. It was dead silent.

She waited a moment, then stuck her head inside. No one here.

A lightweight sweater hung from the back of Gen's chair. Behind it a shelf of business books stood as straight as soldiers. In the corner of her desk Gen's closed laptop had been placed just so. In the other corner was a framed photo of Sylvia, Parker's late wife.

But in the middle of the desk lay a legal pad. It was turned over with a pen across it, disturbing the perfect alignment of the rest of the things.

Overcome with curiosity, Miranda tiptoed around the desk and turned the pad over for a peek.

Gen had drawn a straight line down the middle of the page, making two columns. The column on the left was titled, "Break up with Curt." The other was titled, "Don't break up with Curt." The column on the left had a long list. "Not returning my calls." "Not returning my texts." "Won't talk to me." "Chases after ex-wife."

The second column had only one item. "I think I love him."

Oh, Jeez.

Miranda dropped the pad and ran a hand over her face. If she wasn't mad enough at Holloway already, this took the cake. He hadn't taken her advice about being honest with Gen. He was letting her dangle while he was consumed with his ex. It wasn't fair to the girl. She wanted to shake him and bring him to his senses.

But she had to find him first.

She stepped back into the hall and started to head for the gym when her phone buzzed.

It was a text from Becker. He must be trying to make up for spilling the beans about Iwasaki.

She read the words with a grim smile.

Holloway's at the gun range.

CHAPTER THIRTY-FOUR

Miranda was so mad, she jogged the mile and a half to Aim-Right Shooting Range, which was just down the street from the Agency.

She found Holloway in one of the twenty-five yard lanes. In his goggles and earmuffs, with the thick white bandage still wrapped around his upper arm, he stood at an angle firing into a line drawing of a big ugly guy with a pistol.

Bam. Bam. Bam.

He pressed the switch over his head and waited for the target to slide forward to him. Two hits to the heart area, one to the head.

"Nice work," she said over his shoulder.

He put his gun down on the bench in front of him and turned to glare at her. "Did Becker rat me out?"

"He told me where you were."

He shook his head, replaced his target and sent it back down the alley.

Miranda stepped into the booth next to him and put up a plain milk bottle target. She remembered practicing here with Holloway and Becker for their exams back when they were IITs. When they were buddies, friends.

She pressed the button to send it back and took out her Beretta. She placed her trigger finger so it was a little off and fired five shots.

She brought the target back to examine it.

Three shots were close to the red circle, two in the center of what would be the milk bottle's head, none were dead center.

"You always were better than me," she said to Holloway.

For a moment he pretended not to hear. Then he shrugged. "You pulled to the right. Too much trigger finger."

He knew what he was doing on the gun range.

She holstered her Beretta and watched him fire again. Five shots straight to the head. Would have dropped Iwasaki if he could have gotten them off today. But Audrey had been standing in front of the guy.

"He called me 'soldier boy'," Holloway grunted. "I'll show him what that means." And he shot off another five rounds.

"Soldier boy," no wonder Holloway was pissed. But what that phrase meant to her was that somehow Drew knew Holloway was an ex-Marine. Had Audrey told him? Or did he know that before he met her? Had Iwasaki been researching her detective? Or had he known him a long time ago?

"You make any enemies while you were in service, Holloway?"

"What are you talking about?"

"You know what I'm talking about. Guys who had it in for you. Ever get into a fight in a bar?"

"You mean you think that gangbanger knows me? Has some kind of grudge against me?"

"Maybe."

He shook his head and reloaded. "I don't remember anything like that. All I know is next time I see that guy, I'm not going to miss." He fired again, this time all five shots landed square in the target's heart.

Next time. No doubt Iwasaki was somewhere vowing not to miss again, too. But it wasn't going to happen. Not if she could help it. Miranda wasn't going to let Holloway near that guy again.

"More calls are coming in from Crime Stoppers," she told him.

"So?"

"We need your help."

"I need more practice."

She thought about bringing up Gen, but that would only make him want to shoot more. "They're responding to the partial tag number and the vehicle description Erskine released today."

Ignoring her, Holloway kept firing.

"Someone has to have seen the jeep those two were in. We might be close to finding them. Don't you want to help with that?"

He stopped firing, brought up his target, and holstered his Sig. His shoulders slumped as he turned around. "Okay, Steele you win."

It didn't feel like winning, but she was glad he was being more cooperative.

She looked at his wounded arm, then touched the other one. "I'm sorry you're having to go through this. I know it's tough."

He shrugged away from her with a huff. "Let's just go."

CHAPTER THIRTY-FIVE

Parker sat in his office watching search data for the partial tag number on Iwasaki's jeep flicker over his laptop screen.

No matches.

His head ached with the information Fry had given them about the contents of the amber colored bottle Miranda had found that morning. An antidote for scopolamine. And Fry suspected it had been mixed with hallucinogenics. That could mean only one thing. Audrey Wilson had been drugged and manipulated into trying to shoot her ex-husband.

But why?

Was it simply the insane experiment of a psychopath? Someone who decided to use whatever resentments lay buried in a divorcee's heart toward her former spouse and see how far he could take them for his own amusement?

Or was there something more to it?

And Curt Holloway's attitude toward Miranda disturbed him deeply. He understood the young man was feeling passed over by her promotion to head of the team. But his resistance toward her leadership was uncalled for. He had expected better from him. Parker realized he was distraught under the circumstances. Obviously Curt still had feelings for his ex-wife. That disturbed him, as well.

He hoped Gen would find the courage to end her relationship with him. It wasn't healthy. He ached for his daughter.

He hadn't intended to put Miranda in such a position when he'd put her in charge of the new team. He'd expected cooperation from them.

It troubled him she had had to deal with insubordination. But she was handling it well, so far.

He had considered calling Curt into his office and talking to him, but that would only make things worse for her. Besides, if Miranda ever had to run the Agency on her own, she'd have to handle much more than disgruntled employees.

Switching screens on his monitor, he began to review the calls coming in from the police. He scanned through them, making sure nothing had been overlooked. So far none of them held any promise, but if something did turn up, he would make sure to check on the team before Curt did something rash.

As for right now, he had a small errand to run. He got to his feet and left his laptop running.

As he stepped out of his office and went down the hall, he only hoped they could locate Audrey Wilson soon and end this ordeal for all of them.

CHAPTER THIRTY-SIX

Back in the lab with Becker, her wandering detective, and her laptop, Miranda worked the calls coming in.

It was more tedious and nerve-racking than it had been yesterday. Everyone in town seemed to be guilty of the crimes.

"My brother-in-law has a jeep like that," a man with a gruff voice told her. "I always thought he was a little touched in the head."

"It was my ex-boyfriend. I know it," said a woman who sounded like a little girl.

"It was my father-in-law in that jeep," a woman with a smoker's cough told her. "He's got a mean streak."

Dutifully she checked out each of the calls, and of course, they all turned out to be duds. The first clue was that none of the accused were named Drew Iwasaki. The second was none of them remotely resembled the photo of the guy. The callers were just mad at someone close to them.

Who knew there were so many dysfunctional families in Atlanta?

She got up for a break, got a drink of water, walked around the halls, and returned for another hour of fun.

Someone had seen a camouflage-colored jeep parked at the mall near the office a few days ago. The caller couldn't remember exactly when.

Another caller said she'd seen the jeep near the abandoned shopping center Saturday. That could have been them, but the caller didn't have enough information to tell her anything she didn't already know.

Two more hours passed.

She got up to stretch and stroll around the room. Running her hands through her hair, she was thinking about calling it a night when someone from the OT team rapped on the open lab door.

She turned around and saw a big meaty guy. He stood six-six and had to weigh two-sixty. All muscle. Probably was a lineman on his high school's football team. He wore a light blue polo shirt that set off a pair of outstanding pecs and a head full of light sandy curls. Of course, one of Parker's bodyguards would look like that. But he also had gentle gray eyes and shy crooked smile.

"Ms. Steele?" he said in a faint southern accent.

"If you're asking to go home, I was just about to shut things down for the night."

He shook his head. "No, that's not it. I think I've got something."

"You mean a lead?"

"Yes."

"What's your name?"

"Alex Witherby."

Miranda seemed to recall Gen mentioning him once. "Okay, Witherby. What have you got?"

He pointed to the paper in his hand. "This guy says he and his girlfriend saw the jeep in the park today."

"Let me see that." Miranda took the paper from Witherby's hand and read the transcript of the call aloud, while Holloway and Becker gathered around.

"My girlfriend and I were hiking in the park this morning and a camouflage-colored jeep roared past us, nearly knocking us over. I took down the license plate because I wanted to report it. Then we saw it turn off the road near the old ruined mill. We thought it was surveyors looking to restore the place, but then my girlfriend said there was a woman in the jeep who was dressed like a zombie. I thought they might be having some kind of Halloween party in the woods."

"Was that Sweet Water Creek?" It was Parker's low somber voice that uttered the question.

Miranda looked up, glad to see him standing in the doorway.

"I heard we'd gotten a lead. This is it?"

"Yes, sir," Witherby said, straightening his back as if coming to attention.

Holloway and Becker straightened, too.

"It's right here. I asked him for the name of the park, and that's what he said." Witherby took the paper and handed it to Parker.

He read it over. "He's talking about the ruins of the old Manchester Mill."

Miranda didn't know the place. "Doesn't sound like a very good spot to hide."

"No, it doesn't," Parker said.

She turned to Becker. "Can you pull up the location on your map?"

"Sure can." Becker went over to the counter and swiped and pecked at his tablet for a moment. Then he set it down again. "Here it is." He pointed to the spot.

Miranda studied the digital map with the red dots marking the locations they knew Drew and Audrey had been, and the new dot marking the place the caller had reported.

She pointed at the screen. "The park is ten miles east of the perimeter. Almost twenty miles east of the quarry where the movie's being shot."

"In other words, nowhere near the places we've been looking," Parker said grimly.

Iwasaki had been playing them again.

"Clever of you to plot those points on the map," Parker said to Becker.

"Thank you, sir."

Miranda took the paper back from Parker. "We need to call Erskine and let him know what we've found."

He frowned. "He'll want to take a SWAT team out there tonight."

It was late, but maybe that would give them the element of surprise.

"We should go with them," she said to Parker.

He nodded.

"I'll take my car," Holloway said.

Miranda spun around to him. "No."

Holloway looked stunned. "What do you mean, no?"

"I mean I want you to stay here."

"What?"

She couldn't help thinking about what happened to him on that movie set today. If Drew or Audrey got another chance at him, they just might kill him. Besides, he was in no shape to go on a stakeout.

"I need clear heads," she said to him. "There will be enough police there."

Holloway's face took on a desperate look. "You're shutting me out? Some crazy gangbanger is giving my ex-wife mind-control drugs, and I can't help find him?"

Miranda folded her arms and set her jaw. "You heard me, Holloway. Besides, this might turn out to be another dead end. Stay here and keep monitoring the calls. Or better yet, go home and get some sleep." He'd been going since early morning.

He stared at her as if she'd just set herself on fire. "Like hell, I will."

And he brushed past her and out the door.

"Holloway!" She rushed after him, racing down the hall toward the back, until she caught up. "Stop for a minute."

He halted and turned to her, his face flushed, his eyes wild and bloodshot. "This is my ex. My life!"

That was the point. "I gave you a direct order, Holloway."

"So?"

"So I'm supposed to be in charge, here."

His whole body stiffened. He glared at her with an expression she'd never seen on him before. "You can't order me around anymore, Steele. I quit."

And he yanked open the door to the back staircase and disappeared through it.

Giving up on him, Miranda started back to the lab and met Parker halfway.

She buried her face in his chest, not caring if anyone saw her. "I don't know what to do, Parker. I can't stop him. He won't listen to me."

He ran a comforting hand over her back. "I'll deal with him later. For now we know where he's going. And we're going there, too."

"Right." She raised her head and took a deep breath. "I'll make the call to Erskine on the way there."

CHAPTER THIRTY-SEVEN

Drew burst into the lab and ran down the ramp, his head spinning. Strange blurry colors were forming at the edges of his vision.

He slammed himself over the counter. "You've got to help me, Phin. I've lost the antidote."

Phineas sat with his back toward him, his spine board straight, staring at his computer screen. Through the haze Drew could see he didn't have his ear buds in, so he knew he'd heard him.

That morning after returning from the movie set and locking Audrey in her cell, Drew had gone straight to his room and fallen into bed, exhausted. He'd slept for hours—all through the day and into the night—unable to wake, tossing and turning with bizarre, sickening dreams. When he finally did wake up, he barely knew where he was.

Then he remembered he hadn't taken his "medicine."

He reached for the bottle of the stuff on the nightstand and realized it was gone. He had no idea where it was. But he knew where he could get more of it. He'd forced himself up and staggered to the lift and through the maze of halls, wondering if he'd make it to the lab in time.

And now this kid was ignoring him?

"Phin!" he shouted.

Slowly Phineas turned around in his chair. "You screwed up—again."

Drew put a hand against his pounding forehead. "Okay. I know. It didn't go exactly as planned, but—"

"You're on the news again. The police are after us. They saw your jeep leaving the movie set." He jumped up and slammed his hands on the countertop. "How could you be such an imbecile?"

Hot rage surged through Drew's whole being. The colors began to swirl around in his head. He grabbed Phineas by the lapels of his damn lab coat and dragged him across the counter until they were nose-to-nose.

"What did you call me?"

Fear on his face, Phineas struggled and gurgled a little. "Drew, you're choking me."

Drew twisted the cloth tighter. "Get me the antidote."

"You can't have mine."

"Give it to me now."

It wasn't in his lab coat pocket. Where did he keep it? He'd beat it out of him if he had to.

As if he were reading his mind, Phineas squeaked, "There's an extra bottle, but it's the only one."

He'd settle for that. "Give it to me."

Drew let him go and watched him straighten his coat as he moved to the fridge. He opened the door and took out the familiar small brown bottle.

Drew could see the dozen or so similar bottles of the Elixir stacked neatly on the shelf above it. He came around the counter and snatched the bottle out of Phin's hands. He twisted off the small cap.

"Not too much," Phineas warned. "Just two drops."

"Three." Drew pulled out the dropper, slung back his head and counted them off. One. Two. Three.

"That's enough."

He was right. The stuff was toxic. Drew closed his eyes and took a deep breath. He waited a few minutes. Slowly the dizziness and the colors faded away.

But his anger remained. He glared down at Phineas. "I think you owe me an apology."

"We don't have time for apologies. We've got to make an escape plan."

"Escape plan?"

"The police are looking for us. They released a description of your jeep and a partial tag number to the reporters. Everyone in the area is looking for us."

"We're safe here. No one can find us."

Phineas began to pace back and forth between the cages. "We should dump the girl and make a run for it. We might be able to get into the mountains and cross into Tennessee without the cops spotting us. We can't risk stealing another car. Can we get another tag somewhere?"

"Phin."

"It would only take a few more hours for us to get back to the commune from there."

"Phin."

"What is my grandfather going to say? What is your great-uncle going to say? Our Benefactor won't like it at all."

Drew grabbed him by the shoulders. "Phineas. We're going to be okay."

"Oh, are you as sure of that as you were of that shooting today?"

This kid was annoying the hell out of him. It wouldn't take much to choke the bastard. He'd like to see his eyes bulge and watch him gasp for air the way he did a moment ago.

But he needed him.

He let him go and spoke calmly. "If the cops get near this place, we'll know. Don't you have a police scanner?"

"Of course. I've been monitoring it along with the news channel." Phin waved toward his laptop screen and the 3D image of a radio on it.

"That will give us plenty of warning."

"But what about—"

Before Phineas could finish, the image on the screen began to crackle.

They raced over to it.

A scratchy male voice came through the speakers along with the static. "Unit ten proceeding to Sweet Water Park..."

Then came a woman's voice. "Possible location of male and female suspect in this morning's shooting at Bellwood Quarry..."

Then another man's voice. "Unit twelve on route now."

Phin's lip quivered as he stared up at him. "Did you hear that? They're coming, Drew. They know where we are. They're coming for us."

For the first time, Drew thought Phineas might be right. He felt a tingle of fear ripple through him. Then he shook it off. He wasn't going to be taken down by the cops again. "Don't we have hidden security cameras in this place?"

"In most of the halls, but—"

"And didn't my great-uncle insist on installing some nifty defense mechanisms in the corridors? Don't you remember designing them with him? They're a real death course."

Phin pressed a hand to his head, his brain calculating the odds. He nodded. "Okay, you're right. It's an advantage."

"Plus you've got the war room. If anybody gets in, we'll see them long before they see us. We can control everything from there."

"Right. Right." He still didn't seem convinced.

Phin had never used the war room, but Drew had. It had a whole wall of computer screens. The security cameras fed video to them twenty-four-seven. They'd never had any breach so far. Bored with monitoring the system, Drew had used the screens to play games. It was a way cool setup.

"So we can defend ourselves here a lot better than we can on the road."

Phin looked up at him, his eyes pleading through his thick glasses. "What about those detectives?"

"What about them?"

"What if they're with the police? What if they come after us?"

"Then we'll get the job we were supposed to done."

Phin turned a little pale. "We were only supposed to kill the one. Parker and Steele weren't supposed to even know about us."

He was such a coward.

"So? We'll kill them all."

"Our Benefactor won't like it."

"What are you talking about? He'll be ecstatic. Besides we have our secret weapon."

"The girl?"

Nodding he took a bottle of the Elixir from the fridge and started out the door to the prison rooms. "And this time, I'll make sure she doesn't miss."

CHAPTER THIRTY-EIGHT

It was after midnight when Parker's Mazda pulled past the gate and into the park, followed by a bevy of cop cars. Reaching the end of the road before their escorts, Miranda got out of the car with Parker and retrieved a couple of maglites from the trunk.

"Shall we wait for them?" Parker asked, gazing back at the first squad car, which had cut its lights.

Miranda shook her head. "We can't spare the time. They'll catch up."

"We'll have to walk to the site." He pointed toward a dirt path strewn with fallen leaves.

"Lead the way."

They had to hike half a mile down the trail in near darkness to find the place. The night air was cool and a little windy. As they went along, above them leaves fluttered in the tall trees and drifted to the ground. Owls hooted in the branches, as if calling out a warning.

The trail was wide enough for a jeep, but any tracks had been distorted by forest debris or footprints of hikers by now. At last, they approached their destination, and Miranda could hear the rushing of a nearby stream.

"Here it is," Parker said.

They were standing along a chain-link fence. Parker ran his maglite over the structure looming beyond it. Miranda did the same. There was something there, but she wasn't sure what she was looking at.

Then a cloud moved from behind the full moon and lit up the view.

At the end of a rocky wall stood a stone arch with a wooden frame that looked like it had once been a large entrance. Stretching to the side of the arch stood tall burnt-out spires of old rust-colored brick walls, like spikes pointing up into the dark sky under the moonbeams. Rows of hollowed out rectangles that had once been windows dotted the wall. Moving her light along the length of it, she could see more jagged spikes.

But there was no building. Only an empty frame.

"This is no hideout," she grunted.

"Not on the surface."

Did he think there was something they weren't seeing? The whole case had been like that. They couldn't tell without a closer look.

Behind them the creek ran noisily over a rocky bed. Before them, the chain-link fence ran around the building, protecting curiosity seekers from falling bricks, no doubt.

She eyed the bobbing flashlights of Erskine and his men as they approached up the hill.

Reaching them first, Erskine took in the situation. "Technically, we'd need permission from the state to go in there."

Miranda didn't like that remark. "You get that, Lieutenant. Parker and I will meet you inside."

And she handed her maglite to Parker, put a foot in a link in the fence, and slung a leg over it.

On the other side she let herself down and brushed off the dark work clothes she'd been wearing since that morning.

"You coming?" she said to Parker.

Handing her the lights, Parker climbed over the fence in his expensive suit as deftly as a leopard.

He turned to Erskine. "Lieutenant?"

"Private investigators," Erskine huffed under his breath. "Let's go men."

"We'll check out the back," Miranda said. She didn't want to wait for them all to get over the fence.

Swinging their flashlights back and forth over yet another leaf-strewn path, she and Parker picked their way around the edifice, breathing in the earthy smell of forest and ruins.

"This structure was built in the late eighteen-forties," Parker told her as they went along. "It was financed by some of our most illustrious citizens."

"Including one of your ancestors?"

He nodded. "My fifth great-grandfather, I believe. The surrounding land was home to a hundred workers. It was five stories, the tallest building in the area at the time."

"What happened to it?"

He gave her a thin smile. "Sherman."

So it had been war that had ravaged this place. She looked up at the full moon casting its eerie light against the burnt-out spires of the ancient structure. For a moment it reminded her of Tannenburg's house in Evanston, Illinois. She'd passed out there, and when she woke up she'd thought a falling beam had hit her on the head. But it wasn't a beam. It was Tannenburg. He'd snuck up behind her and choked her until she passed out.

She could still hear his voice in that musty basement where she'd found him much later. "Don't you remember the feel of my arm around your neck?"

A chill went through her.

She shook herself. No time for reminiscing now.

They had reached the back of the structure. But she still couldn't see any signs of life. Just the hollow shell of the burnt out building, its floor covered with undergrowth.

"Nobody could keep a hostage here."

"No," Parker agreed.

"Wait." She ran her flashlight over the ground in front of the back wall. It illuminated the corner of a square shape that seemed to be made of concrete. "What's that?"

She moved to it, rustling through the leaves until she reached it.

She squatted down and found a mat made of artificial foliage covering the spot. Something hunters would use for camouflage. But it wasn't completely covering what it was hiding.

She pulled the mat up and tossed it aside. Underneath lay the square concrete slab whose corner she'd spotted.

Fixed atop the square sat a round shape. It looked sort of like a large manhole cover, but it had hinges at one end and a handle on the other. If this were part of the mill, she'd expect it to be rusted and broken. But this thing looked brand new, and like it was made of galvanized metal.

Not a material available in the late eighteen-forties.

Parker came over to her side and bent down to run his light over the slab. "Definitely not part of the original construction."

"Are you thinking what I'm thinking?"

"That it's some sort of entrance?"

"Yeah, sort of a hatch. But to what?" She didn't want to think about what was running through her mind.

"If so, it's probably locked from the inside." Parker studied the handle, no doubt assessing his lock picking skills against it.

As she waited, Miranda noticed a path through the leaves that led across the backyard and up a hill thirty or so feet away. She shined her light in that direction. At the top of the rise, if she was seeing it right, the fence had been cut away.

"Look at that." She started for it.

Leaving the mysterious manhole cover, Parker followed her.

She hurried across the dirt, climbed the steep incline, and ducked under the fence through the hole. She was in the forest now, tall pines and oaks thick around her, blocking the moonbeams. Overhead night birds cawed in the branches. But a few yards ahead she could make out an odd shape.

Walking toward it, she raised her light. It revealed a large mound covered with leaves and a tarp.

She moved to the rear of it and lifted the corner of the tarp.

There it was. The rear bumper. Camouflage-colored. The tail light. And the first part of the tag number.

PQA52.

Her insides turned icy. "He's here," she whispered to Parker.

"Yes, he is."

What he didn't say, she knew, was that he hoped Audrey was still alive.

Parker went to the front of the vehicle and pulled up the tarp to see if anyone was inside. Just as he leaned into the driver side window, Miranda heard a scraping sound coming from where they'd been a moment before.

She turned around and saw a tall lanky figure lifting the manhole cover by the handle.

It wasn't locked, after all.

"Holloway," she hissed and started after him.

"Miranda," Parker's commanding voice rumbled behind her.

But she couldn't turn around.

She had to stop her detective from going in there. She had to warn him. But she wasn't fast enough. She scrambled back under the fence and down the hill just as Holloway disappeared into the hole.

She couldn't let him go in there alone. She ran to the cover, lifted it up, and climbed down into darkness.

CHAPTER THIRTY-NINE

Cursing under his breath, Parker raced down the hill and hurried to the concrete opening. What was Miranda thinking?

But he knew perfectly well. She was protecting the detective in her charge. The charge he'd given her. Protocol dictated the right thing to do at this point, the correct thing, was to call Hosea for back up.

But there wasn't time.

Instead he raced to the lid of the opening, flung it open and climbed inside. His foot found a short ladder, then a concrete stair, and his flashlight illuminated the rest of the way. Twenty or so steps downward into the earth.

At the bottom he found himself standing in a short passage with an arched ceiling made of dull brown brick. The construction looked new. At the end of the hall, not more than ten feet away stood a door.

Reinforced steel, so it seemed, Parker thought as he ran his flashlight over it.

This was definitely not part of the nineteenth-century mill. But who had built it? And for what purpose?

His mind raced with the possibilities, but there was no time for speculation now. He had to focus on one thing.

Finding Miranda and Holloway. And Audrey if she was still alive.

They both must have gone through that door. There was no other way out.

Hoping he was right, he reached for the latch. It opened easily, giving him the uneasy feeling they were all heading straight into a trap.

He stepped through anyway, and watched in dismay as it slammed shut behind him.

He was inside a circular chamber about six feet in diameter. The floor was granite. The walls were done in gold. Three gold doors faced him. They were positioned symmetrically at the points of a diamond, taking in the entrance behind him.

As he examined each one, he saw they were split down the middle with a button in the wall on the side. Elevator doors. But there was no indication of floor numbers. Which one had Miranda taken? Which button had she pushed?

As he considered the choice, the doors to his left slid open. Sensing a trap, he remained where he was until they closed again and he heard the compartment descend. He took the door to his right.

But as soon as he stepped inside and the doors closed before him, he knew he'd made a mistake.

There was only one button.

Three elevators and only one button? This place, whatever it was, must have three floors, assuming each of the other elevators went to only one. He had a one-in-three guess that Miranda had taken this one.

The odds were not in his favor.

The trip wasn't long. He could only guess how many feet he had descended. And when the compartment stopped, the doors that opened again were at its rear. His heartbeat picking up and his senses on high alert, he stepped out into a long dimly-lit hall.

Miranda was nowhere in sight. He didn't dare call out for her.

He'd try another floor. He spun around and heard the compartment moving. There was no button for the elevator. Only a pad to place a hand for palm print identification. That was no good to him.

He was trapped.

There had to be another way to the other floors. He'd find a way to get to her. He had to.

Slowly he stepped deeper into the passage and turned on his maglite.

The space was perhaps twelve feet wide and seemed to be the length of a large banquet hall, though he couldn't make out the far end of it. No windows, of course. He was deep underground. Narrow slits of light mounted near the ceiling revealed flat stone walls with no adornment. The floor was a similar monotone tile material that echoed as he walked. The air was cool and had a slight mineral scent.

Not good.

He took a few more steps and stopped to listen. He could hear something. A slow whirring sound. And he felt a slight vibration.

Before him lay a large oriental carpet of light and dark browns. The pattern was Isfahan, if he wasn't mistaken. Costly. But then so was this whole underground structure. He thought of Iwasaki's gang connections. Built by drug money?

It would certainly be a good place to store and distribute their goods. And that would explain the elaborate security measures. But what did that have to do with the substance Fry had found in that amber bottle?

No time to work through it.

Something was under that rug. He bent down and lifted the corner. It was loosely secured to the floor by tape. He gave it a hard tug. It was lighter than he'd thought, and he nearly lost his balance as he tossed it aside.

When he saw what was under it, he was glad he'd caught himself.

The floor had been hollowed out, and in the large pit below was a succession of spinning pipes mounted with dozens of deadly sharp spikes. Punji sticks, made of shining steel instead of bamboo. If he had stepped onto that carpet, it wouldn't have held. He would have gone down with it, and would have been caught between two of the spinning pipes, and stabbed and sliced viciously until he fell through to whatever lay below. It would have been a slow painful death.

Had Miranda fallen down there?

He shined his flashlight into the pit, straining his eyes. He could see no blood. The pit was perhaps ten or twelve feet deep. There would be a body at the bottom if she had failed to cross it. But who had replaced the carpet?

No, she must be on another floor. Or she'd escaped this trap somehow.

He turned and shined the light on what he had grabbed onto for balance a moment earlier.

A row of embedded metal rungs went all the way up to the ceiling and continued across over to the other side of the pit. Another set along the wall descended to the floor. The safe way across.

Could he trust them to hold?

He'd have to. Shoving his flashlight into his belt, He took hold of the first rung and began to climb. Up he went, then across, hand-over-hand until he'd reached the other side. He dropped to the floor and was relieved to find it solid. He used his light once more to check for blood on the tiles or a body in the pit from this vantage point.

He saw nothing.

He turned and peered down the long cavity before him. There was no exit at that end, but there had to be a stairwell somewhere. Something that led to another floor. He just couldn't see it from here.

He took two steps toward the far end. Something shot out from the wall right in front of his face.

He ducked just in time to miss a long sharp blade.

His chest heaving, he dared to rise. He touched the blade. It was real enough to put out an eye or worse. He studied the shape and curve of it. A katana. Japanese samurai sword. Katanas and metal punji sticks. Iwasaki was harkening back to his heritage.

Parker ran his hand over the wall. No laser. He looked up, using his flashlight. Ah, there. In the corner of the ceiling he could just make out the edge of a hidden camera. Someone was watching.

Still, he'd have to take his chances.

He took another step and another katana shot from the wall. He sidestepped it and moved to the middle of the passage. Another katana flew up from the floor. He leapt away, but not before the blade cut into the slacks of his suit. No, it wasn't just his suit. He could feel the sting on his shin and knew he was bleeding, but he couldn't stop to tend it.

And then he noticed a painting along the opposite wall.

Taking his light again, he studied it for a moment. It was a fierce black Japanese dragon with huge talons and a ferocious fur-like crest. There was another beside it. And a third.

Before Parker could contemplate the significance of the design, a blast of fire shot out from the first creature's mouth.

He ducked just before the flames consumed his face.

He pivoted in a squatting position and was about to rise when another burst of flame came from the opposite wall about two feet from the floor. He jumped up as high as he could, feeling the heat on his toes as he missed it. He came down hard on the floor.

Dear Lord. Who could have built such a demonic obstacle course? Someone with a juvenile imagination and a great deal of money. And a love for video games.

He'd make a run for it, he decided.

But as he rose from the floor, a whizzing disk flew through the air toward his head.

He ducked in time, but it sliced the top of his shoulder. More blood. Again he tried to get up and run. Another spinning disk flew toward him.

Ninja stars, he thought as he ducked again. Before he could move another one whizzed past his head, nicking his ear. He rolled, got up, jumped and dodged the vicious stars all the way to end of the passage.

By the time he reached it, he had multiple cuts to his arms and legs. And his suit was shredded.

He couldn't think about that now. He threw himself against the wall. It opened into a hidden passage, and he fell to the floor in complete darkness.

Stinging from his cuts, he reached for his flashlight. Relieved he hadn't lost it in the melee, he switched it on. And then he saw what he'd been hoping for.

A concrete staircase descending downward.

He got up and hurried down it.

CHAPTER FORTY

Miranda felt her way along the rough cave-like wall, her flashlight in her free hand, wondering what in the world had happened.

She'd thought Parker would be right behind her. She'd heard him call out for her just as she went down the manhole. By the time she'd reached the golden elevators, she thought he'd catch up to her, but he hadn't.

That had disturbed her, but she couldn't wait. A door to her left had opened and she'd taken it, assuming that was the way Holloway would have gone. But she'd seen nothing of him, either, since she'd been wandering around in this damp-smelling catacomb.

She should stop and make her way back to the elevators. Try to find Parker and get Erskine and his men down here to search for Holloway. But she had no idea where she'd come in.

She was lost.

Who installs golden elevators in an underground cave, anyway? Somebody rich. Somebody with a sadistic imagination. The same type of person who would use mind-control drugs on a young woman desperate to become an actress.

Her fingers were getting raw from feeling her way along the jagged rock. Overhead the rock became an uneven arch. Beneath her was more rock, slippery with moisture. The tunnel seemed to go round and round in circles. It had to have been hewn out by some boring machine. How did Iwasaki, or whoever was funding him, manage that without anyone seeing them?

Money, again.

They must have paid the crew top dollar. They must have had guards of some sort posted to shoo away any curious onlookers. And if anyone higher up was asking questions, they'd be bought off.

Could a Los Angeles gang pull that off? She didn't think so. This was bigger than that.

Screw it, she thought. Holloway wasn't down here. She'd have to find her way back to those elevators. She turned around and felt for the other side of the cave. She followed it back to where she thought she had been, but the craggy walls didn't look familiar.

Of course, everything here looked both alike and different.

Swallowing down the urge to panic, she moved on. She'd gone about fifty feet when her fingers touched air.

She turned her head and saw there was another passage, a fork forming a tunnel to the right and one to the left. The one she had come down?

Maybe. Or had she passed this way already?

A tingle went down her spine. This was the way. She was sure of it.

Drawing in a breath, she headed down the fork on the right. Around a corner, the landscape changed. There was light here. And smooth walls with ninety degree angles at the ceiling instead of the irregular dome of hewn rock. Shiny linoleum on the floor. Walls freshly painted in eggshell white. Everything looked brand new. Drab, but new.

And looking suspiciously like a hospital wing.

Up ahead she saw a door along the hall that looked like it might lead to a patient's room. She put her flashlight away and hurried toward it. She tried the latch.

Locked. No window to peek inside.

Two car lengths away was a second door. She hustle over and tried it. Also locked.

She spotted another one across the hall and sprinted over to it. No luck with this one, either.

Was anybody in these rooms? Or were they awaiting fresh victims? Was Audrey locked in one of them?

She didn't have her pick set with her. She hadn't thought she'd need it on a movie set. She put a hand to her head. It had been nearly twenty hours since she'd gotten dressed that morning. It seemed like years ago.

But a curving passage lay before her and there were more doors to try. She did so, one by one. Finally, she reached the last door at the end of the hall. If this one didn't open, she'd go back and find Parker. He had to be here somewhere.

She put her hand on the latch and felt a sensation that was both strange and familiar. Like caterpillars crawling up her back, plaguing her nerves with their delicate legs and hairy bodies.

The girl with the gift.

Holding her breath, she pushed down the door handle. It opened easily.

What she saw inside made her heart stop.

This was no hospital room. It was more like a prison cell with cinder block walls, a single bed, no windows, and little furniture. But it was the smell that hit her the hardest. Like the sensation she felt, it was all too familiar.

The rank rotting of human flesh.

Miranda put a hand over her nose and mouth to fight down the inevitable nausea.

On a thin mattress on a plain bed frame lay a young woman. Her skin glistened with ruptured blisters, but she hadn't begun to bloat yet. A few flies had found their way into this fortress and were buzzing around the body. Her eyes and mouth were open toward the ceiling, as if she had been screaming, begging to be spared from some unimaginable agony.

Miranda instantly knew who she was from the bloody stub at the end of her right foot. Her big toe was missing.

This was Rebecca Duncan, the twenty-six-year-old homeless girl whose toe she'd found in the abandoned mall off Memorial.

Her head began to swim. She had to find Parker. She had to get Erskine and his officers down here now.

She turned and ran back down the hallway.

CHAPTER FORTY-ONE

Drew clasped his sides and rocked in his chair as he convulsed with laughter. He couldn't help it. This felt so good.

Still laughing, he wiped the tears away with his knuckle and watched the screen again. "Look at that, Phin! Look at him jump."

They were in the war room, watching the action on one of the huge computer screens.

Phin's whiney high-pitched nerd laugh rang in his ears.

Drew slapped Phineas on the back and took a swig from his hard cider bottle. He pointed to the screen. "Look, he's bleeding."

"We almost got him!" Phin cried as if he'd just scored a hundred points.

"We did." Drew giggled again. He couldn't help himself. He hadn't had this much fun in a long time.

Wade Parker, the high and mighty ace detective of the southeast, was dancing to their tune now, he was completely at their mercy. Just like when they were kids throwing rocks at squirrels in the woods and giving themselves points for the best shot.

"He's good," Phineas said. "Are you sure he won't get through?"

"Of course, I'm sure. He won't last much longer. Switch to Hall Two."

Phin pressed some keys and the tall skinny Curt Holloway appeared on the screen, weapon drawn, he inched cautiously down a dark corridor.

"He's searching for Experiment Two."

"And he'll find her soon." Drew had to giggle again.

"You've got her primed?"

"Locked and loaded and buzzed to the hilt. Wait 'til you see it. She's going to rip him apart."

Phin glanced at a screen to his side. "The cops are still rummaging around outside."

"Doesn't matter. We'll handle them, too. But first, I'm going to take care of this one." Drew reached over Phin's shoulder and switched to the view of the Prison Hall and the dark-haired woman running.

"She found the body."

"And now she's heading for the lab."

"Just as we planned. Miranda Steele has met her match." Drew got to his feet, drained the rest of his bottle and tossed it in the trash. Then he picked up the bottle of the Elixir and wiggled it in the air before he slipped it into his pocket. "And here I come, ready or not."

"Just don't screw it up."

"Like I keep saying, you worry too much."

CHAPTER FORTY-TWO

"Stop and think. This way," Miranda muttered to herself as she turned down another passage. But where that elevator should have been was another wall.

A dead end.

She turned around and made her way back. She should have counted her steps when she left the elevator. She should have made notes in her phone, but she'd thought she had her bearings.

Not anymore.

There was a light up ahead. At least she could see the walls of the cave now. She could hear a generator running somewhere. It looked so familiar. This had to be where she'd come in.

She didn't like closed in spaces like this. She felt as if the walls were closing in on her. They couldn't actually do that, could they? She wasn't sure. She'd been up almost twenty-four hours. She was tired and disoriented. But she couldn't stop now. Not that she had a choice.

At last she reached the end of the tunnel. The light she'd followed was suspended over a sliding door.

No knob or latch. She felt along the walls for a control panel. She found a button hidden behind a recess in the rock. She pressed it, and the door slid open. She stepped through it into a wide, brightly lit hall.

But there were no elevators here.

Here the walls were high and straight and lined with sheet metal, giving the hall an industrial look. A steel ramp lay before her. A safety rail had been erected along one side of it. At the end of the ramp lay about ten feet of linoleum like the floor of the hospital-like area she'd found earlier.

In the middle of the wall was a large steel door with rounded corners.

It looked thick, as if it barred entrance to a place where dangerous experiments were conducted. Like mind-control experiments? The idea set her nerves on edge.

Across from her lay another ramp matching the one she stood on. It too had a door like the one she'd just come through.

She heard a creak and realized the door was opening. A figure stepped through it and came down the incline. He stopped at the bottom staring straight at her.

She recognized him from his picture. Black eyes. Pure black hair. Smooth, unblemished complexion. Dressed in his black leather jacket. But he was taller than she thought he'd be. And more muscular. And meaner looking.

Drew Iwasaki.

His lips parted in a sinister grin. "Hello, Ms. Steele. So happy to meet you. Especially under these circumstances."

The mockery in his tone made her ill and angry.

She nodded toward the steel door between them. "Is Audrey Wilson in there?" she demanded.

He just stood there, staring and smiling.

"I've already found Rebecca Duncan."

He chuckled, as if he knew that. As if he'd planned for her to find the homeless girl. He took a step toward her. "Don't you want to know about your husband, Wade Parker? Don't worry. We're taking care of him, too."

What did that mean? Iwasaki knew Parker was here. But where was he? Did Drew know about Holloway? Fear rattled through her. And rage. If this bastard had done anything to Parker, Erskine was going to have to arrest her for first degree murder.

He started up the ramp toward her.

She reached into her waistband and pulled out her Beretta. Aiming it more accurately than she had at the gun range earlier, she watched him stop in his tracks.

"Let's try this again. Tell me where Parker and Audrey Wilson are."

His black eyes glowing, he eyed her hungrily. "My, aren't we brave? But you won't shoot me. Without me, you could be lost down here forever." He started up the ramp again.

"I'll take my chances. Get back or you'll wish you did."

He let out a sickening high-pitched giggle. "Oh, you aren't going to use that weapon on me."

He had a point. She needed the information this creep had. She should shoot him in the leg instead, but he was close now. Harder to get that angle.

Still, she lowered the gun, aiming for his kneecap. Before she could pull the trigger, he lunged forward fast as lightning, reached for her wrist, gave it a twist.

An Aikido move. She knew it from sparring with Parker. Aikido was his specialty, along with several other martial arts. But that didn't keep her from letting out a yelp of shock.

She kicked out at Drew's leg, tried to wrap her foot around his shin to knock him off balance and bring him down. She knew martial arts too. But as she struggled to hold onto her gun, his thumb dug into the tender crease of her wrist, loosening her grip.

She gritted her teeth against the pain.

And then he pulled her over.

Down they went, tumbling over each other. The gun flew out of her hand and skittered across the metal ramp.

Damn. She was blowing this. Her instincts were off. Probably from wandering around disoriented for so long. And from lack of sleep.

But she wasn't going to let this creep get the best of her. She was better than this.

As they rolled toward the railing, she pulled her arm back and jabbed as hard as she could. Her fist landed square on his jaw, and she thought she heard a snap.

His dark eyes turned to flames. Grabbing her throat he rolled her over. "I was going to let you live, bitch. But now you've changed my mind."

"Me, too."

She pressed her hands together, pushed them between his forearms and snapped them apart. Her fists became motors. She pulled herself up and smacked at his face again and again like it was a punching bag in the gym. He tried to fight back but he had to cover himself with his hands and roll away. She freed herself of his body and began to crawl down the ramp to her gun.

Inches before she reached it, Drew recovered and grabbed her leg.

She tried to shake him off. "Let go of me, you bastard, or else."

"Or else what?"

Tightening her stomach muscles, she raised her torso as high as she could and lunged for her gun.

Her fingers touched the handle. Struggling with all she had, she worked the weapon toward her hand. Drew began to pull her away by her leg. But she had it. She had her gun.

She lifted it from the floor and spun around. "Or else this."

She fired into the wall. The bullet pierced the metal behind him, making an inch deep dent.

Staring at the damage, Drew let her go and scrambled to his feet.

Miranda got to hers, holding the gun on him.

"You can't do that," he cried.

"I just did."

"You bitch, you."

"Now, you're going to open that door."

His chest heaving he glared at her. He glanced once toward the door. Then he leapt into the air. His leg came up so lightning quick, she barely saw it before it slammed into the side of her head.

Again she fell to the floor. This time her gun flew all the way across to the other ramp.

Damn, he was good, she thought, her head ringing and burning with pain. She blinked hard and forced air into her lungs. He hadn't knocked her out. She still had her bearings. He wasn't going to get the best of her again.

He came at her again, as she knew he would, and just before he lunged, she raised her knees to her chin and kicked out as hard as she could.

Two could play at kickboxing.

Her feet struck him hard in the chest. His eyes bulged with surprise as he flew across the hall. The back of his head hit the railing with a loud clunk, and he slid to the floor in a heap.

Out cold.

Miranda scooped up her Beretta and scrambled to her feet. She raced to the thick metal door and studied the control panel.

No telling which button would open it. She'd try all of them, if she had to. But at the first one she pressed, the door slid open.

There was another ramp here. She moved down it and stared at the huge space. The air was cold and smelled of disinfectant, strange chemicals, and—something living. The sterile-looking floor was marked with yellow-and-black warning tape. There were fluorescent lights and huge shafts crisscrossing the high ceiling. Cages were stacked along the walls with small animals in them.

Above the hum of what must have been a generator, she could hear their scratching and soft moans.

Were these—experiments?

She stepped farther into the room and saw microscopes and laptops scattered over a countertop. This was a lab.

Was this where Drew had cooked up that inky black substance in the amber bottle she'd found? Was this where he'd concocted his mind-control drug?

No, he couldn't have done all this alone. There was someone else.

She peered over the counter and stopped in her tracks.

Beyond the counter was a chair. A strange looking contraption that reclined back. It had straps hanging from the arm and leg rests. And long wires near the headrest that seemed to be attached to a nearby machine.

Her blood went cold.

Was that what she thought it was?

But no one was in it. No one was in here.

She risked another step forward. "Parker?" she called out.

No one answered. Audrey wasn't here. Parker wasn't here.

She saw a shadow flicker across the floor. Someone was behind her. Was it Drew or his accomplice? Before she could turn around, a hand clamped over her mouth and nose.

Another hand slithered around her neck like a snake. An elbow flashed before her face. The hand at her mouth moved to pull the elbow tight, making the arm squeeze tight against her carotid arteries.

Years of training had her kicking out behind her, using her own elbows against the attacker's torso.

But she wasn't fast enough. Her blows were weak, powerless now. She didn't have enough air. Her head began to spin.

Rear naked choke. She'd been in one before. That time Parker had gotten her out of it. Where was he now? Was he dead?

He must be, or he'd be here.

As her heart began to sink with despair, so did her body.

The lights above her seemed to flicker, then dance in her brain. She felt her muscles go loose as she slid into the strong arms.

He lifted her up and everything went black.

CHAPTER FORTY-THREE

Silly girl, Drew thought as he took the gun out of her limp hand, stuffed it into his belt, and carried her body around the counter.

The back of his head and his jaw ached from the blows she'd delivered, but he liked that she'd given him a challenge. Did she really think she could beat him? She might be good, but he'd been trained in Aikido and Taekwondo and Karate since he was five years old.

It was going to be so much fun to bend her will to his.

He carried her over to the chair and laid her gently on it. He began strapping her into it. Three straps on one arm, three on the other, three for each leg. He pulled them tight. Had to be tight for this one or she might get up too soon.

He let out a giggle as he eyed the electrodes connected to Phineas's machine. That was where the boy genius administered shocks and recorded the brainwaves of their human experiments. That would be an interesting study, something even he'd be intrigued with. But Phin was busy having fun in the war room.

Besides, he had his own plan.

He took her gun from his belt and laid it on the counter just where she could find it. He was debating whether to use the gag when the door behind him opened and Phineas ran into the lab.

He hurried to the counter. "Drew, we've got to get out of here."

"What are you doing in here, Phin? You're supposed to be manning the controls."

"Didn't you hear me? We've got to leave now." He eyed the new experiment in the chair. "Just leave her and let's go."

Drew rolled his eyes. "What are you rattled about now?"

Phin waved his hands in exasperation. "The police. They're coming. They've found the front door."

"Just do what you did to Wade Parker."

"I can't, Drew. They've disabled the controls."

That couldn't be right. They had backup generators. And the lab ran on a separate one. He had to be exaggerating.

Phin glanced around the room like he was insane. "We have to get out of here."

Drew gestured to the woman in the chair. "Phin, this is my masterpiece. See that over there?"

Phin turned toward the countertop. "That gun?"

"Right. It's her Beretta. I'm going to have her shoot Wade Parker. Won't that be a hoot? Don't you want to stay and see it?"

His eyes wide behind his thick glasses, Phin shook his head. "We can't do that. It's too risky. Just kill her. Kill her now. Give her an overdose of the Elixir. If we can get to the commune, they won't find us."

"What are you worried about?"

"About the rest of my life," he screeched. "I don't intend to waste my genius in a prison."

"We aren't going to prison. My great-uncle will see to that."

"I don't think so. Not this time." He grabbed Drew by the arm. "Are you coming with me?"

Drew shook him off. "Not until I finish here."

"I'm not staying here, Drew."

"Do as you please."

"I'm taking the jeep."

"Whatever."

Phin stared at him a moment as if he'd lost his mind. Then he scooted around the chair and hurried out the back door.

"Coward." The kid didn't understand what kind of power they had. He was too much of a nerd.

He'd finish his game here, then head back to the war room and take care of any police that might have gotten in.

Drew reached for the Elixir in his pocket. But first, he pulled out the antidote and put two drops under his tongue. He didn't want to end up like he had the other day.

He put the antidote back and took out Phin's home brew. He looked down at the woman in the chair.

Her eyes were fluttering open.

"Ah, there we are," he said to her.

Then her eyes flashed with horror. Her face turned a lovely pale shade as she realized where she was. He loved the first expression when they woke up. It gave him such a rush.

She began to struggle, just like the other two had. But this one was feistier.

"Get me the hell out of here," she grunted.

Drew laughed enjoying the sensation of power. "Now why would I do that?"

Her heart pounding with panic, Miranda stared up at her captor. She eyed his smooth skin and pure black hair. His black eyes had no feeling at all in them.

She gritted her teeth. "You're going down, Iwasaki. The police know you're here. They know who you are and what you've done."

He snorted. "Is that supposed to frighten me?"

"You may have been able to escape prison before, but not this time. This time you'll be sentenced to death."

He let out a disgusting high-pitched giggle. "You are so funny." He leaned in so close she could smell his breath. "Not before you and your husband are dead."

Her heart began to hammer. "What are you talking about?"

He held up a small amber bottle. "See? This is the secret formula. The Elixir. At least that's what I call it."

Her face must have told him she knew what he meant.

"You found my antidote at the movie set, didn't you? That was where I lost it, wasn't it?"

"Antidote?" she said, trying to play dumb.

"It keeps me from going under the spell of this." He held the bottle close to her face.

It looked a lot like the vial she found. "Are you sure you don't have the bottles mixed up?"

"Very clever. But you're wrong. The antidote has a dropper. Two drops under the tongue will keep me safe. I've already taken my dose. But this," he held the bottle up so she could get a good look at it. "This is a spray. It has the scent of a cologne. I've even worn it before." He giggled. "It drives the women crazy."

She glared at him. He was insane. And mad with his own sense of power.

"Nothing to say to that?" he jeered. "I've found helplessness can do that to a person. You see, once I spray you, all the most frightening things buried in your subconscious will come to life. You won't be able to tell what's real and what's not. And then all I'll have to do is whisper in your ear, and you'll do anything I say. You'll think it will make the nightmares stop. But it won't. And when I put that gun in your hand, you'll shoot anyone I tell you to. Even the person you love most."

Like hell. Her chest began to heave. She fought hard to get out of the straps. There had to be a way to get free. "You won't get away with this. If they don't give you the death penalty, they'll put you in an institution for life."

He laughed again and shook his head condescendingly as he twisted off the cap of the vial. "You just don't understand, do you? I'll just have to show you. That's all."

And he raised the bottle to her face. She took a deep breath and shut her mouth tight. He slid his finger over the pump and pressed three times.

She felt the spray as the droplets hit her face.

She closed her eyes and turned her face away. Listening to that ugly sadistic laugh, she held her breath for as long as she could. But she didn't last long.

And when she gave out, she inhaled a big noseful of the horrible stuff. It smelled like honeysuckle and cinnamon—and lethal poison.

At first she didn't feel any different at all. And then the darkness came.

CHAPTER FORTY-FOUR

She plunged down into the deep dark hole.

Down, down, down she went. Swirling, whirling, her gauzy dress billowing all around her. She flailed her arms and legs, reaching out, trying to grasp, to hold onto something. But there was nothing there.

And then she hit bottom.

Her body crashed against the hard floor with a slap. She sat up and rubbed her face. It ached where she'd smacked it against the concrete.

She looked around. Where was she? She reached out and felt the rough surface of brick all around her. Had she fallen down a well? It was so dark. And then she saw a tiny light near the corner of the floor. Like a single brick had been pulled out.

The opening led to somewhere.

Her hands and knees protesting in pain, she crawled over to it. It was so small. She couldn't fit through it. She began to dig at the ground with her nails. If she could make the hole bigger, she could crawl through it.

"What do you think you're doing?" boomed a voice behind her.

Something grabbed her by the hair and pulled her back, dragging her through the opposite wall and into another room. It was a hollow cave-like chamber lined with jagged rock. The light was better here, but still low, and the rocks glowed yellow and orange all around her.

Pain shot through her head, her neck. She struggled to turn around, to get to her feet.

"You stupid bitch."

A heavy hand struck her face and she went down again.

She began to cry. "Leon, why are you doing this?"

"You know why. Because of what you are."

His hand came down again. This time she rolled away and his blow went through air.

"You can't do that to me."

"Yes, I can," she screamed. "Where's Amy. Where's my daughter?"

"You'll never find her, Miranda. You'll never have her."

"Yes. Yes, I will."

He came at her again.

She began to crawl as fast as she could. The rocky surface beneath her cut into her knees and legs. She kept going. There was a way out. An opening in the rocks just ahead. More light there.

She managed to get up and run toward it, but as she did, her feet slipped on the rocks and she slid. Down, down again. Until she tumbled onto a concrete floor.

Slowly she stood to her feet.

She knew this place. The musty smell of it. The candles flickering in the bags against the walls. The air was stifling and she felt herself begin to sweat. Not just from the heat.

A man appeared across the room, half hidden in the shadows. She knew him, too.

"Hello, Miranda. And so we meet again."

"I killed you."

His laugh echoed against the walls, vibrated in her head. "And yet I keep coming back. You'll never be rid of me. Of us." He pointed up.

She looked over her shoulder and saw the body hanging from the rafters. Hands tied over her head, tongue drooping from her mouth, blood dripping from the hundred holes he'd poked into her. Hannah Kaye. The young woman she couldn't save.

"I'm sorry," she whispered up to the corpse.

"Don't be," the man said. "She doesn't deserve it. And neither do you. You'll be joining her in a moment."

He stepped into the light and came toward her. She could see the big muscular shoulders, the shaggy dirty blond hair he wore to his earlobes, and those grass green eyes so full of evil.

He had a rope in his hands.

"And now it's time to take your medicine."

Medicine. Medicine. His voice echoed with the word as if she'd never heard it before.

"Get away from me." She kicked out at him and spun away. Her strength was coming back to her.

"I have your daughter," he said. "Our daughter. I'll always have her."

"Oh, no you don't." She kicked out again, but this time he grabbed her foot and she came down with a crash.

He pushed his body on top of her, grabbed her arm and looped the rope over one of her wrists. She fought, she tried to bite him, but her teeth only went through air.

"No. No. No," she cried, struggling as hard as she could.

And then the ropes came free. Gasping for breath she stood to her feet.

Dizzy, she reached behind her and steadied herself on the arm of a chair. What room was this? It was cool and large and buzzing with the hum of a generator.

Her vision was hazy and bright colors danced before her eyes.

There was a door at the far end of the room. A man stepped through it and came toward her. He seemed to be talking but she couldn't hear him. All she could see was the thick red dots clouding the air.

"It's Leon," a voice whispered.

Was it Leon? She wasn't sure.

"It's him. Shoot him."

It was Leon. She wasn't going to let him hit her again. Shoot him? Yes. There was a gun on a nearby counter. She picked it up and aimed it at him.

"Don't come any further, Leon."

But he took a step anyway. He raised his hands. "Miranda, it's me."

The voice seemed familiar. For a moment warmth filled her heart.

"He's coming for you. Shoot him."

He was. He was almost to her. In a moment he'd be on her. She couldn't let that happen. She couldn't.

She pressed the trigger and fired.

CHAPTER FORTY-FIVE

His Sig drawn and his maglight in his other hand, Curt Holloway made his way down the dark corridor, keeping his back to the wall the way he had since he'd stepped off that elevator.

This was the strangest place he'd ever been in. All the crazy drills and situations he'd experienced during poolee training and boot camp in the Marines hadn't prepared him for this. He'd been wandering down this dark hall for hours. At least, he'd thought it had been hours, but he'd lost track of time.

The walls and floors were smoothly polished black onyx. Someone had put a lot of time and thought into the design. And money. Twenty feet then a ninety-degree turn to the left. Thirty feet and a ninety-degree turn to the right. On and on and on. He had a feeling he was going in circles. He was frustrated to no end.

If they were keeping Audrey in this hall, no wonder she'd been acting so crazy. She must be so frightened.

No, she wasn't crazy. It was those drugs. He'd barely been able to hold it together when Fry explained what was in them.

And then Steele wanted him to stay out of it?

She had no right to do that. When he'd spotted her and Mr. Parker looking at the entrance to this place, he knew he was going down there. When they moved to the top of that hill, he'd decided to take action. But just now, he wished he had waited for them. He'd seen Steele coming down the hill after him. He'd assumed they'd both catch up after a while, but they hadn't shown.

The idea unnerved him.

But he couldn't focus on Steele now. He had to find Audrey and get her out of here.

He came to a stop and tried to figure out what to do next. He thought about the definition of insanity. Doing the same thing over and over and expecting a different result. He couldn't keep going in circles.

On a wild hunch he shined his light on the wall across from him. Look at that. There was a niche in it with what looked like some sort of switch. A large industrial power switch. He hadn't seen that before. Maybe he hadn't been going in circles.

But what did it do? Maybe turn on some lights. That would be good.

He crossed over to it and put a hand on the lever. Feeling the nerves swimming in his stomach, worse-case scenarios went through his mind. Water flooding the hall and drowning him. The walls turning into giant conductors and electrocuting him. A huge ball of flame consuming him.

He'd been watching too many movies.

He couldn't just keep going around lost in this place. He straightened his back and pulled the lever.

None of his imagined scenarios happened.

Instead to his right the wall opened, revealing a long dark staircase. Without thinking twice, he hurried down it, two stairs at a time.

When he reached the bottom, he found another door. He pushed on the handle and it opened to a brightly lit space.

He turned off his light and looked around, blinking. Walls painted in a chalky white. A white floor with a diamond patterned linoleum. A receptionist desk. A curving hall with rooms off to one side.

It was a hospital floor.

Was Audrey in one of those rooms? He hurried across the space and tried the first door. It was locked. He tried the next one. Also locked. He tried the next one and the one after that. No luck.

Frustration burned inside him. Where was she?

Then he heard the sound of a monitor beeping. And someone crying. Audrey. She was in here somewhere. He knew it. He just had to find the right door.

But just as he reached for the next latch, he heard a door open at the end of the hall.

He looked up and saw a figure emerge from a room.

She was barefoot and dressed in a hospital gown. Her hair was ratty and uncombed with a bad case of bed hair. Her eyes had that glassy look like the last time he'd seen her at the movie set.

And in her hand was a semiautomatic handgun. Stainless steel. It looked like a .44 Magnum with maybe ten rounds.

She started for him.

"Audrey," he cried out to her. "I'm here. I'm going to—"

She raised her arm and fired the gun.

Holloway ducked just as the bullet blew a hole in the wall a foot over his head.

"Audrey, honey. Don't do that."

She fired again.

He ducked behind a metal service cart. The bullet whizzed past him. Her aim had gotten better.

"C'mon, baby. Put that down and let's go get some pizza."

Again she fired.

This time the bullet hit the cart, spinning it away from him and making it sing. He raced across the hall and dove behind the receptionist desk just as she got another round off.

He could try to make her spend all her rounds, then rush her, but that was too risky. Talking was no use. He'd have to try something else.

She fired again, and the tray spun around and rolled toward him.

She'd been firing at the sound of his voice. Maybe the drug messed up her vision. He had an idea. There was a glass vase full of artificial flowers at the end of the desk.

He picked it up and hurled it against the opposite wall. It hit high and shattered into a thousand pieces with a loud clink.

Audrey turned and fired at it just as he thought she would, blowing another big hole in the wall. Before she could turn back, he positioned the cart and gave it a hard shove. It rolled down the aisle and hit her square in the knees.

She stumbled, confused, and lowered the gun.

He rushed forward, shoved the cart aside, grabbed her weapon arm with one hand, and put his other around her waist.

"What are you doing?" she cried, sounding like a frightened child.

She pulled back and they tumbled to the floor. She tried to fight him, kicking and biting, but his attention was on the gun. He held her wrist and shook it hard until she let go.

Then he picked up the weapon and slid it down the hall as far as it could go.

"Let me up. Let me go." Audrey kept kicking and pounding on him with her fists.

He spread his legs over hers to stop the blows, then he put his body over hers as best he could. He used an elbow against her neck to keep her teeth away while he reached into his pants pocket.

He drew out the small glass bottle he'd been carrying. Back in the Agency lab, he'd talked Becker into getting it for him when Steele was out of the room. It wasn't the original bottle. It was one that belonged to the Agency.

Becker had poured off just enough of the antidote into it to work, according to Fry's speculation.

He hoped Fry was right.

And that Audrey wouldn't knock it out of his hands. He struggled to open the bottle and squeezed the stopper to draw up the liquid. He put it to her lips.

She turned her head away.

"C'mon, baby. Do it for me. Please?"

As if he'd finally made sense to her, she opened her mouth. Was that the programming Iwasaki had done? It didn't matter now.

Carefully he let two drops fall into her mouth. He lifted her jaw to shut her mouth, put the cap on the bottle, and waited.

Slowly she stopped fighting him. Her blows grew light and finally her arms and legs went limp on the floor. She lay there for a long moment, her eyes closed. Was she breathing? Fry had said the stuff was toxic. Had he killed her?

Then her chest expanded and she opened her eyes.

She looked at him like he was a space alien. "Curt? What are you doing in my apartment?"

Her voice was normal. She was back. He wanted to cry with joy.

"We're not exactly in your apartment."

Pushing him off of her, she sat up and looked around, alarm on her face. "Where am I? What is this place?" She looked down at her hospital gown. "And what the hell am I wearing?"

"This is a bad place. I'm going to get you out of here. C'mon." He got to his feet and held out a hand to her.

Still looking bewildered, she took his hand and began to follow him. "I'm going to be late for rehearsal. I got the part of Mrs. Gibbs in Our Town. Did I tell you?"

"I heard about it."

He led her out of the hospital room and into an open space that looked like a cave. Now he wasn't sure where he was.

"Where are we going, Curt?"

"We're getting out of here. Just give me a minute to think."

But before he could decide what to do, he heard a loud clang. It rang out again. Bam. Bam. Bam. The sound of metal against metal.

He took out his flashlight and shined it against the wall about ten feet away. Large chunks of rocks began to fall from the surface.

Bam. Bam. Bam.

Someone was breaking through. He didn't know whether to run or go help them. He took out his gun and pushed Audrey into a corner, shielding her with his body.

"Who is that, Curt?"

"I don't know."

But the answer came quickly enough. The battering ram punched its way through the wall and a man dressed in a SWAT uniform stepped into the cave. Behind him were two other officers, and Lieutenant Erskine.

"Over here," he shouted, holstering his gun.

Erskine hurried toward him. "Holloway, are you hurt?"

"No. I'm fine. I've got Audrey. She was drugged. She didn't mean to do any of those things. I gave her an antidote. The one Steele found at the movie set. She's better now."

But Audrey had that bewildered look again. She was frightened.

"What are the police doing here, Curt? Am I in trouble?"

Erskine's face turned grim. "I'm afraid we're going to have to take her in."

"I know. But she's innocent. I'll swear to that in court."

With a nod of acknowledgment Erskine gestured to one of the officers to take Audrey. "We'll let her speak to the staff psychiatrist."

Audrey grabbed onto his arm. "Curt, what's going on?"

"It's going to be all right, babe. I promise. Just go with this officer now."

He hated to let her go, but at least she was safe from that madman now.

As the officer led her out through the hole they'd made, Erskine turned back to him. "Where's Iwasaki?"

"You haven't found him?"

"No. I thought you did. And Parker and Steele? Aren't they with you?"

Curt felt as if the floor were sinking beneath him. "I haven't seen either of them."

CHAPTER FORTY-SIX

Parker leapt behind a counter as the round from Miranda's Beretta buzzed past his head.

He'd had a bellyful of flying objects whizzing around him by now. He'd had to fight his way through no less than three halls of spinning Ninja stars and shooting flames and swinging scythes before he'd found this lab.

His suit was in tatters and his body felt just as shredded. But that was nothing compared to the terror of what he saw before him now. It was another trap. The most vicious and sadistic one of all.

As he stared at her in shock, his heart crumbled like an imploded building.

Miranda stood behind the counter of this lab aiming her gun at his heart. She had a bruise on her cheek and blood on her suit. She'd been fighting, but she'd lost.

Behind her stood a wicked looking chair. Some sort of place where Iwasaki subdued his victims, no doubt. Parker could see by the glazed look in her eyes, Miranda had been his latest one.

Iwasaki had gotten to her.

He'd given her that damn potion. Scopolamine. And whatever hallucinogenics were mixed with it. God only knew what it had done to her brain. She was the love of his life. He couldn't lose her like this. He wanted to tear Iwasaki apart for doing this to her.

But he knew he had to focus or she'd kill him soon.

She was coming around the counter now. She walked with slow, deliberate steps. Her eyes moved unnaturally, as if she was seeing only a half of what was before her.

Zombie brain, Fry had called it. His gut twisted inside him at the thought.

He pressed his back against the bottom of the counter. A wooden stool hid him partially from view.

He tried not to breathe, but she must have heard him anyway. The drug hadn't lessened her keen abilities. She aimed and fired, blasting a hole in the wall not three inches from his head.

He had to do something now.

He grabbed onto the stool and swung it across the floor, aiming for her legs. If he could knock her down, there might be enough time to get to her before she fired again.

As if she sensed it coming, she stepped to the right, almost dodging it. It slammed against one leg, stunning her just long enough for Parker to draw out his Glock. He couldn't reach her in time. This was the only way.

Hating himself, his heart sinking into quicksand, he rose and took aim.

He had to be accurate. If he wasn't he could hit an artery or worse. Once more she raised her gun.

They stood there for what seemed like an eternity, weapons pointed at each other.

Parker lined up his sights with the edge of her arm.

Before she could pull the trigger again, his jaw set, he fired.

The shot was good. It hit her just where he needed it to, grazing her upper arm.

With a look of shock, she stumbled back, but she didn't drop her gun.

He holstered his Glock and rushed toward her.

Pushing her back, he wedged her against the wall.

She fought him hard. She had always been a good fighter and was even better after being with the Agency, but he could subdue her. He hoped. Still, he winced as she kicked against the cuts on his legs.

"No. No," she murmured, as if half asleep.

Patiently he wrestled the Beretta out of her hand, enduring her kicks and punches. He'd endured enough of them through her many nightmares. Her eyelids were closed now. Beneath them, her eyes moved back and forth in a REM-like state.

He could only imagine the horrors playing through her mind now. She must think he was Leon. Or Tannenburg.

"Miranda," he said softly. "It's me."

"No!" She kept on fighting him.

But he had her gun now.

Pressing her hard into the corner, he pinned her with his hips and legs. He slipped her weapon into his pocket and removed the amber bottle he'd taken from the lab before they left the Agency tonight.

It was a miracle it hadn't been smashed to pieces by now, but it was intact.

He placed his elbows against the walls on either side of her head and held the bottle over her. Her hands beat against his arms, making it hard to hold onto it. Her head rolled back and forth as she snapped at his arms with her teeth.

It would be a trick to get the liquid into her mouth. Especially if she bit him. And if he dropped the bottle—

Struggling to escape his hold, she pressed her hips against his, arousing desire and urgency within him. Most inappropriate feelings at such a time.

But his mind went back to the first time he'd sparred with her in the

Agency gym. They had ended up on the mat doing much more than sparring. He remembered dropping her off at her apartment the next evening and pressing her against the column outside her front door, need nearly consuming him. A little like now.

He glanced up at the bottle and thought about Fry's warning.

It was the only way.

As steadily as he could, he twisted the lid off the bottle, filled the dropper full and put it to his mouth.

He squeezed three large drops onto the tip of his tongue and pressed his lips hard against Miranda's. He forced his tongue into her mouth and delivered the dose, stroking the sweetness of her until his breath grew ragged and he could barely stand it any longer.

Praying the mixture would work, he continued his assault.

She grunted and growled into his mouth, trying to escape, but after a moment the blows against his arms and legs grew softer. He felt her muscles loosen. At last the grunts melted into a moan of desire. She slid her arms around his neck and kissed him back.

She was here again. She was coming back to him. The potion had worked. Thank God. Oh, how he'd love to make love to her right now.

But they had to get out of this dreadful place.

He forced himself to pull away from her and watched her eyes open. They were normal now. That gorgeous vivid blue and those deep dark lashes that had captured his heart the first time he saw her.

She blinked and frowned at him as if waking from a dream. "What are you doing here, Parker?"

"Giving you what you needed." He stepped back and twisted the stopper back onto the bottle.

Miranda stared at the amber vial in Parker's hands, confused images racing through her mind. "Was I—? Did I—?"

Then she saw his suit. It was cut to pieces. Parts of it were hanging off him. He was bleeding. "Did I do that?"

"Our host did that," he said darkly.

Host. Iwasaki.

She glanced around at the room. Her breath turned shallow. "That chair. He put me in it. Did he use that stuff on me?"

Parker's solemn look was enough to tell her the truth.

"That bastard." She patted her waist. "Where's my gun?"

"Unfortunately, I had to take it from you, my dear." He pulled it out of his pocket.

Her eyes went round. "Did I—try to shoot you?"

He held the gun out to her. "You're better now."

She put her hands to her face. "I tried to shoot you like Audrey did Holloway? Oh, my God."

She couldn't believe it. What was in that potion that could make her want to hurt Parker? She put a hand to her head. It ached in a way it never had before.

For a moment, she thought she might heave.

Then she remembered being in that chair and Iwasaki telling her what he was going to do to her.

She snatched the gun from Parker's hand and stuffed it into her waistband. She'd find him and make him sorry for everything he'd done.

"I haven't had any luck finding Audrey or Curt," Parker said, eyeing her carefully.

He was worried about her condition, but she felt fine now.

"Me, either. I found Rebecca Duncan's body, though."

He nodded grimly. "We need to find a way out of here and get to Erskine. We need more manpower to scour this fortress thoroughly."

"I'll never forgive Holloway for leading us down here."

She pulled her hair away from her face, wondering how they were going to find him. Then she heard a back door close at the far end of the room.

Iwasaki.

Her whole body came alert. "That sonofabitch was here, watching us."

"So it seems."

She stepped around Parker and took off.

"Miranda," he said, caution in his tone.

She couldn't wait. Ignoring his warning, she scrambled across the room, past that awful chair, to the door. She had to get that guy.

She pressed a button on the wall, and the back door slid open to a well-lit corridor. She ran down the passage until she reached an elevator. Was this the way she'd come in?

Who knew?

She banged on the button until the elevator opened. Parker was just coming around the far corner.

"I'm going to the top," she cried as the doors closed before her.

She pressed the inside button, and the elevator deposited her in the golden circular chamber where she'd come in. She slammed down the latch on the reinforced steel exit door and was relieved when it opened for her. She raced through the brick passage with the arched ceiling, hurried up the concrete stairs, climbed the ladder, and found the hatch that led to the outside.

She pushed it open and breathed in fresh air. She climbed out and got her bearings.

The sun hadn't risen yet and the bright moon was low in the sky. Blinking hard, she could just make out a figure rustling through the leaves toward the hill at the far end of the property.

It was Iwasaki, all right. The coward was running away.

Not if she could help it. She pulled her Beretta from her waistband and steadied the sights. He was moving fast and her vision was still a little blurry, but she didn't have time to second guess herself.

She aimed and fired.

Dirt and leaves flew up near his kneecap. She'd missed.

Try again.

But he'd stopped. Turning back toward her, he raised his hand, his own gun in it.

This time she aimed for his chest. Standoff? She thought. Not with this guy. Whoever fired first would win.

That was going to be her. She pulled the trigger.

Click.

She was out of ammo.

Still peering through her sights, she could just make out the corner of Iwasaki's lip as it turned up in satisfaction. She watched him steady his weapon.

Hit the ground, she thought. But before she could, a loud blast rocked the air. Iwasaki's body jerked to the side and went limp. He dropped the gun, fell to the ground, and rolled down the hill covered in leaves.

Parker? She turned her head. No, not Parker.

Standing ten feet away from her with his Sig still extended, was the brown suit and tall lanky frame of Curt Holloway.

CHAPTER FORTY-SEVEN

Miranda watched one of the SWAT officers who'd come around to the back of the ruins at the sound of gunfire. He was on the hill, examining Iwasaki's body. Another officer was climbing the hill to the spot where they'd found the camouflage-colored jeep.

Holloway shuffled through the leaves and stood before her and Parker, who had climbed out of the manhole just in time to witness his feat.

"I found Audrey," he explained. "Then Erskine and his men broke into whatever that place is down there and found us. When they took Audrey out to one of the squad cars, I went with her. But they wanted to talk to her alone, so I came back here to see if I could find you."

"Guess you showed up in the nick of time," Miranda said. "You saved my life, Holloway."

He shrugged. "I couldn't let him kill you. And it was a good excuse to pay him back."

"Good thing you got in that extra target practice."

He answered with a half-grin.

Parker extended a hand. "Excellent aim, Detective. Thank you."

Holloway gave Parker's hand a stiff shake. "You're welcome."

"I hope this means you'll reconsider tendering your resignation," Parker said.

Holloway put his hands in his pockets and looked down at his feet. "I think I'm going to need some time off after this, sir."

"Oh?"

"Audrey needs me."

Miranda looked at Parker. Audrey was going to jail. She might have been under the influence of her captors, but she'd need to prove it to a judge first.

"Ms. Steele?" the officer on the hill called out.

Miranda started toward him. "Yes?"

"Is this the spot where you saw the jeep?"

Miranda climbed the hill with Parker behind her. "That's the spot."

"Yes, it is," Parker agreed.

"It's not here."

The three of them trudged up to where the officer stood. Miranda retraced her steps, Parker confirmed this was the correct place. They stood together in the small clearing surrounded by pines. This was definitely where she and Parker had seen the jeep before they'd gone down into the tunnel system.

But there was nothing here now except the tarp lying on the ground and a few tire tracks in the pine straw and leaves.

"Someone else was here with Iwasaki," Miranda said, her body tensing.

The officer started down the hill. "I'll have Lieutenant Erskine put out another BOLO on that plate. We'll find him."

If the other guy wasn't smart enough to take the tag off once he got somewhere he could stop.

"I'll go with him," Holloway said. "I want to check on Audrey." And he scampered down the hill and around the brick ruins.

Miranda put her hands to her face. "What are we going to do now, Parker?"

He slipped his arms around her and pulled her close. "You've been up twenty-four hours. We've both been through hell. I'm going to take you home, feed you, and put you to bed."

She looked down at the gash on her arm, then at Parker's torn and bloody suit. "And maybe put something on these wounds?"

"Yes. That, too."

She closed her eyes and rested her forehead on his strong chest. "That sounds wonderful."

CHAPTER FORTY-EIGHT

Two days later Miranda got up extra early and texted Mackenzie to see if she wanted to go for a run before school. She picked her up at the Chatham mansion, and they went to their old trail in Chastain Park.

With her long dark hair pulled back in a ponytail, Mackenzie had on black tights, a pink sleeveless quilted jacket-vest, and new pink-and-blue running shoes. Miranda was happy her parents took care of her every need.

They did some warm-up stretches, then took off on the five K path.

The air was crisp and cool, and the oak trees along the path were a burst of color with their flaming orange and red leaves. As they jogged along, Miranda drew in oxygen and relished how clear her head felt. She peered through the evenly spaced trees trunks. Not a zombie in sight. And best of all, she was spending time with her beloved daughter.

After three miles, they stopped to cool down.

"How's the anti-vaping project going?" Miranda said as they strolled along.

"TAV," Mackenzie corrected.

"Yes, TAV. How's it going?"

"Okay. Not as many kids have signed up as I had hoped. Donations are sparse."

Mackenzie's speech seemed to have impressed the adults. Didn't mean it would have the same impact on her peers. It might have the opposite effect.

But Miranda wanted to be supportive. "Maybe it'll pick up later."

Mackenzie started to walk a little faster. "I just have to put more work into it."

Right. Picking up her pace, Miranda decided to change the subject. "You'll be turning fifteen next month."

"Yes, I will."

"And so will Wendy. I can't believe it."

She could still remember holding the tiny baby in her arms when she was just three weeks old. Of course, there was nothing to remember after that. She'd missed Mackenzie's childhood, though Colby and Oliver had shared pictures of Mackenzie growing up with Miranda. She'd appreciated their generosity, but it wasn't the same.

"So what do you want for your birthday?"

"I don't know. I haven't thought about it much."

Something else on your mind? Miranda wondered.

She caught a yellow leaf in her hand as it drifted to the ground. She twirled it between her fingers as they walked, a little slower now. "It's funny. I've always had trouble with this time of year. More winter, really. But fall means winter's coming."

"Is that so?" Mackenzie kept her gaze straight ahead. She didn't ask for details like she once had.

Miranda forced herself to continue. "It must be hard for you now, too—after what happened last year."

She lifted a shoulder. "I try not to think about it."

Is that what all these projects were about? Was she keeping herself too busy to think about what Leon had tried to do to her? Miranda knew that wasn't Dr. Wingate's advice. She didn't think keeping things buried was healthy.

"Do you want to talk about it?"

"About what?"

"About Lake Placid. I went through it, too, you know."

For a long time Mackenzie walked along in silence. It was as if she were building a wall between them. Then she pointed toward the street where cars were parked. "Oh, there's Rachel."

"Rachel?"

"Rachel Alex. She's a junior at school. She's interested in TAV. We've been discussing ideas lately, and we've sort of become friends. I asked her to pick me up, and there she is."

She let out an awkward laugh and started for the car, as if she couldn't escape fast enough.

Taking a long step, Miranda reached for her hand and turned her around.

The girl scowled at her in surprise. "What are you doing?"

"Mackenzie, it's not good to avoid your feelings. I know. I did it too long."

Miranda watched her cheeks color. Whether from embarrassment or anger, she couldn't tell.

She shuffled her feet and looked away. "You know, Mother, I'm going to be really busy with my schedule and my extracurricular activities and all for a while. I'm not going to be able to get together with you much. Maybe I'll see you during the holidays. Mom wants to do something, I think."

She looked down at the hand Miranda was still holding onto.

Miranda let it go, not knowing what else to say.

"Gotta run." Mackenzie gave her an artificial smile, then turned and hurried toward the waiting car.

She was definitely hiding something. Not that they'd ever been able to talk about the past. Or anything, really. But Miranda was more certain than ever that deep down Mackenzie was troubled.

And she didn't think it was just about Lake Placid.

CHAPTER FORTY-NINE

"I don't know what to say," Parker said quietly.

It was after lunch and Miranda was sitting next to him in the Mazda as they drove down Piedmont heading south. She'd just confessed to him how she'd bombed out with Mackenzie that morning.

She shrugged. "Not much to say. I guess I'll have to wait until she's ready to tell me what's bothering her."

"I wouldn't stop trying."

"No. But for now, I think I need to give her some space."

He was quiet for a moment, then he changed the subject. "I spoke to Hosea earlier today. He and his men are still going through Iwasaki's underground lair."

Her hands clenched involuntarily at the mention of that place. "A lot to go through and catalog."

Parker nodded. "They found a cache of handguns, explosives, and teargas. And a control room where Iwasaki and his accomplice must have watched all of us on hidden cameras. They also controlled the lights and their 'games' from there."

Miranda shuddered remembering what Parker had told her he'd been through in those dark halls of horror.

"The chamber of commerce, the Conservancy staff, and even the governor are aghast at the lax security that allowed something like that to be built under a historic landmark."

"Right under their noses." She let out a smirk. "Bet they're all pointing fingers at each other."

"That's putting it mildly." He made a turn onto the ramp to I-85, heading toward Midtown. "One of the first things Hosea did was to take those caged animals Iwasaki and his unknown accomplice had been experimenting on to a shelter where they can be restored back to health and found homes."

"That's good." She'd felt so sorry for those poor creatures. She knew what they felt like.

His next words were low and ominous. "Hosea is calling in the GBI and FBI to help process all the evidence."

FBI? She turned to face him. "Parker, someone with a lot of money had to finance that project."

"Yes."

She thought about Simon Sloane and The Custodians, the organization they'd run into during the Dylan Ward Hughes case. Sloane had sworn her and Parker in as agents, but she assumed that had expired by now.

"Group 141?" she said softly.

The name Sloane had given the Ukrainian syndicate he'd thought was running a kidnapping ring. But they had found only one Ukrainian at the scene. A big man named Doroshenko. The FBI had taken him into custody, and she and Parker hadn't heard any more about him.

Parker gave her a meaningful glance. "Possibly. There's no way of knowing yet."

Except your gut. Was someone—after them? That seemed so farfetched. But so was that underground labyrinth.

Turning onto Peachtree, Parker changed the subject. "Audrey's arraignment is set for next week. Curt wants Estavez to represent her."

"Is he going to?"

"He's thinking about it. Even so, the mandatory minimum for attempted bank robbery is ten years."

"Estavez will get her off. He can work magic." Almost as well as Parker could.

And their testimony would help, too. After what she'd gone through, she'd be happy to tell a judge about the experience. And so would Parker. And, of course, Holloway.

"Are you giving Holloway the time off he requested?" she asked, glad Parker hadn't made her make that decision.

"I'm going to give him two weeks."

Miranda nodded. She straightened her slacks and decided to ask the sensitive question. "What about Gen?"

Parker drew in a long weary breath. "She told me she's going to break up with him."

"Oh." Miranda thought about that note pad on her desk. *Poor girl.*

"She said she feels as if she's been dating a married man."

Miranda didn't blame her. She couldn't figure Holloway out, even if he did just save her life. "That's probably the right decision."

"I hope so."

Wanting to think of something more pleasant, Miranda returned to her phone and the sites for luxury car dealers she'd been looking at.

So far they'd been to four different dealerships. They'd looked at two Ferraris, three Porsches, and countless Lamborghinis.

Parker didn't like any of them.

Why was he being so picky? At this rate they'd never find a replacement for his ruined sports car.

"How about an Alfa Romeo? The 4C Coupe looks pretty cool."

And it was more in her price range than the half a mill the dealer had wanted for the sleek silver Aventador at the last place they'd visited. But she was bound and determined to get Parker a new car if she had to pay most of her salary for the rest of her life.

"I'm thinking of something else. Maybe in red."

Red? That was more her color.

He took a turn onto 17th, then went left on Techwood.

Hey, she thought. This was near her old apartment.

They passed a fire station and a church she recognized.

"I think we should stop in here." He turned into a drive along a chain link fence and a sign boasting low monthly payments.

"Here?"

It was a used car lot. Not where Wade Parker the Third bought his vehicles. Then she looked around. Wait a minute. She knew this place.

"In fact, I called the dealer earlier. He has a model I think you'll find particularly interesting."

He drove around the beige brick building, past the garage and the lot full of clunkers, all the way to the back.

And there parked in a spot with no other cars around it was a very familiar looking red sports car.

Her mouth fell open in shock. "Is that my Corvette?" The ZR1 she'd traded in for rent money after she'd left Parker?

"I believe it is."

She sprang out of the Mazda and rushed over to the tapered side. She ran her hand over the curved hood. Smooth as glass. Freshly polished. The tires were new, too. She hadn't realized how much she'd missed it.

Parker strolled over to her with a smug look on his face. "I bought it back shortly after the case in Jasper County. The dealer was kind enough to hold it for me."

Her mouth still open, she gave him a punch on the arm. "You sneaky devil. You've been keeping it here all this time?"

His gray eyes grew tender. "I was waiting for the right moment."

A skinny man in a bold green jacket ran out from the main building, a huge smile on his face. "She's in great shape, Mr. Parker. Just as you ordered." He held up the keys and dropped them into Miranda's hands.

Her heart full, she stared down at them. She was getting teary-eyed. "You want to give me this, even after I tried to kill you?"

Parker chuckled. "You could only do that if you left me again."

And he didn't mind saying it out loud. But she never would. She'd never leave him or try to kill him again.

She suddenly felt so happy, she didn't know what to do. Not caring that the dealer was watching, she put her arms around his neck and let him swing her around in the air.

"Whee!" she cried, feeling lighter than she had in weeks. "I'm the luckiest girl in the world."

CHAPTER FIFTY

It had turned cold today. The temperature had dropped and the weather people were predicting snow by the end of the week.

Nonetheless he pulled on his coat and left his office on the fiftieth floor of the Sector Building. He rode down the elevator to the parking deck, and got into the back of the limo.

The driver took off, heading west on Essex Street. It wasn't his regular driver. It was a man from his other enterprise. Someone he could trust.

As much as he could anyone.

As they drove along, he stared out the window at the old brick buildings of Boston and thought of his mother. He'd never known who his father was, but his mother had been a sweet, kind woman. A simple and very beautiful woman. A giving woman. She'd worked as a clerk in a medical office doing menial grunt work, never wanting more. They got by, but barely.

He remembered the cramped little apartment in Mission Hill he'd grown up in. He thought of how she used to take him in her arms and comfort him whenever the bullies at school would tease him about his worn clothes.

He had loved her very much, but he never could understand how she could be so content with so little. And then when he was eighteen, she developed a brain tumor and died within a year. He'd gone to live with her sister in a commune in Kentucky. It was there he met the people who would change his life.

There he learned what possibilities lay before him.

He wanted more than his mother ever had. A lot more. He wanted everything. And now there was an opportunity that would put him beyond the richest men in the world. Billions were at stake.

Except there was Doroshenko. If he talked, he could lose everything. The organization could lose a great deal, as well. And he would no doubt be running for his life.

He reached into his pocket for an antacid tablet and slipped it into his mouth. The stress was eating away his stomach lining.

The assassination attempt he'd had executed two days ago had failed miserably. He'd had to put down the man who hadn't been able to deliver. The guards would be on alert from now on. The mission would only get more difficult. For now, all he could do was hope Doroshenko understood what the attempt on his life meant and keep his mouth shut.

And now this.

They drove for another hour heading south, well away from the city. After a long excursion through a rural area, the driver turned into a park where the trees were dense. They drove over a rough dirt path to a picnic area near a small lake.

When the limousine stopped, he got out of the car and walked down into a small valley where the fall colors were dazzling, despite the overcast sky. The dry leaves crunched beneath his feet as he went. The late morning air was chillier than he'd expected, and he pulled his double-breasted topcoat around him as he took his place. The driver standing just behind him, he waited.

Soon another limousine appeared. It was black, like his own. It parked beside his and after a moment a man exited the rear door and made his way down the same path.

His dark trench coat rippled in the wind as he walked and ruffled the dark patch of graying hair atop his head. But his perfectly trimmed black goatee remained in place. He was as fastidious as ever.

The man came to a stop three feet away from him and bowed.

He almost felt something for the man who had given him guidance and wisdom after his mother died.

But he only nodded in reply. "Iwasaki. You have a report?"

"Yes, sir. The boy is well. Shaken, but unharmed. He made it home to our leader. He abandoned the vehicle when he got to the mountains. He walked to the next town and called us from a payphone he managed to find at a local store."

Iwasaki looked at him as if he expected a reply.

"He is terribly sorry for failing," he added.

It was a failure. When he thought of the millions he'd poured into that underground facility in the south…now gone. There would be no return on that investment.

Iwasaki bowed again. "He wants me to say he begs your forgiveness."

Forgiveness? For the devastating loss he'd suffered? A two-year setback? That he could not grant. But the boy was unusually intelligent and gifted in the skills he needed right now. He would let him live. And thankfully, he had other facilities to turn to.

"Regrettably, my great-nephew was a different story," Iwasaki continued.

Watching the grief in the man's eyes, he let him go on, telling him what he already knew. The Atlanta police had breached the secret underground facility and rescued the woman he had targeted for them to experiment on. They had gathered evidence of the activities that had gone on there. And worst of all, one of Wade Parker's detectives had killed Iwasaki's great-nephew. The detective who was supposed to have been shot to death in the bank robbery while Wade Parker and Miranda Steele were out of town.

He never should have let Iwasaki handle this mission. That had been an error in judgment he would not make again.

Iwasaki was still babbling. "We have learned from this setback. Yes, it was costly, but the lessons are valuable. We will try again. We will not fail next time."

A twinge of regret pulled at his heart as he took the semiautomatic pistol from his pocket.

As if involuntarily, Iwasaki's hands went up in surrender. He opened his mouth, his face full of shock, his goatee still perfectly shaped around his mouth and chin.

"You must give us another chance. The boy has such promise. He swears he will—"

He fired three bullets straight into Iwasaki's heart and watched him fall to the ground.

He studied the body a moment, then turned to his driver. "Clean up this mess."

"Yessir."

He strode back through the leaves to the limos and went to Iwasaki's first. He tapped on the driver's window and waited for it to roll down.

"Yes, sir?" said a trembling voice.

"Tell Bach to be more careful next time."

"Yes, sir." The window went back up and the engine started.

He watched the limo roll away, then climbed into the back of his vehicle to wait for his driver.

His plan to take out Parker's team of investigators one by one would have to be scrapped. Apparently they stuck together like a family. He'd have to take them out as opportunity presented itself. And in a way that didn't draw attention. The new plan would take some thought.

He would have to wait a while for them to let down their guard, but he would be back.

And next time, he would not fail.

THE END

ABOUT THE AUTHOR

Writing fiction for over fifteen years, Linsey Lanier has authored more than two dozen novels and short stories, including the popular Miranda's Rights Mystery series. She writes romance, romantic suspense, mysteries, and thrillers with a dash of sass.

She is a member of Romance Writers of America, the Kiss of Death chapter, Private Eye Writers of America, and International Thriller Writers. Her books have been nominated in several RWA-sponsored contests.

In her spare time, Linsey enjoys watching crime shows with her husband of over two decades and trying to figure out "who-dun-it." But her favorite activity is writing and creating entertaining new stories for her readers.

She's always working on a new book, currently books in the new Miranda and Parker Mystery series (a continuation of the Miranda's Rights Mystery series).

For alerts on her latest releases join Linsey's mailing list at www.linseylanier.com.

For more of Linsey's books, visit her website at **www.linseylanier.com**

Edited by

Editing for You

Made in the USA
Middletown, DE
26 March 2022